Bachelors Road

Candyce Lange

DEDICATION

To my father, who was in love with a lake
for sixty years

CONTENTS

ACKNOWLEDGMENTS

To the long-running 'London Group'
and the 'Black Buoy Writers' in Wivenhoe,
who all worked on this collection, and to my siblings
and Michael, who listened and never wavered

STEELE, 2010

Jerry had been supplying Joe Steele with fresh water for the last month. Steele was a skilled mechanic when it came to boats and motors, but his water pump had stayed broken all summer. It was a matter of Steele's pride, the way they didn't talk about it. My brother Sam told me the story as we drove up to Cross Lake. I was visiting from England, where I lived, for my summer holiday and Sam had coordinated his truck-driving job so he'd be here for my last week.

'The Bachelors', they called themselves, all more or less camping on The Point. Sam was the only one who wasn't a Vietnam vet and the only one who lived in a house, though it was a work in progress. Jerry and Dwayne lived up the road in reinforced steel trailers with trucks and boats and old snowmobiles parked outside. Dwayne worked away sometimes. Jerry mowed grass in the summer and drank in the winter. Steele owned the tiny dark green cabin by the crossroads near Red Eye Resort. He was the most aloof, though I'd spent an afternoon with him two years before. Oh, they all nodded hello or waved politely when I was out on the bicycle, but they lived on the edge in ways I didn't understand.

Sam and I stopped for supplies on the way up. 'We don't need too much food,' Sam said.

'Yes, we do,' I answered. 'We'll be here a few days.'

So he bought ingredients for sweet and sour chicken, his favorite dish, and ice tea in bottles and I bought breakfast cereal and cinnamon rolls because I knew that with all that fresh air and exercise I'd need something to get my teeth into.

When we stopped at the liquor store, he said, 'No cheap wine.'

I shrugged and paid for a big white and a small expensive red, and he bought beer and Kahlúa, which is what he drank when he was truly on vacation. I knew he stayed totally sober when he was trucking; we'd been talking about Black Russians on the way up and how long it had been since he'd tasted one. He'd pushed his baseball hat off his forehead and joked about what a connoisseur of vodka I used to be and I laughed because these days it was an occasional pint in a pub back home, and it was water I needed. I couldn't wait to swim and then climb into clean pajamas and eat dinner with the sun going down.

It was a tradition, when we arrived at Angel's Pond, to slow down and take stock of the lake, take a look at the cabins, wave if you saw anyone but mostly we didn't. Mostly it was the lake and the wind and the trees and the fish and cranes and maybe loons or eagles. It was their wild and interesting place and I loved it because it didn't change much.

When the storm started, Sam came down to the dock to call me out of the water. And so the first night we were forced to stay inside and talk to each other.

I put silverware and plates on the island counter in his kitchen and watched the yellow sky out of his high windows. I'd found a few candles, which I lit. Sam stood at the stove stirring his sweet and sour. He looked lean and fit and was telling me about the air pressure of clouds against the heat of the lake. Forty years ago he'd majored in Geography in college, and he liked to remind me that he still studied the weather the same way I edited every sign and menu I saw. I was pretty disheartened by the misuse of the apostrophe; he worried about global warming and the lake being fished dry.

'Our obsessions,' I said. 'Do we ever change?'

'I'll tell you what I'm obsessed with. Making some money so I can finish the bedroom upstairs. That means' – and he pointed the wooden spoon at me – 'my bed is still packed in the garage and that couch is on its way out. So I'm sleeping in the den and you're sleeping in the truck.'

Just like him to wait and tell me. But I didn't mind. Sam loved being on the road, but I knew it had to be lonely at times and he'd go days without a normal conversation or a real meal.

So we ate while the storm died down, then we moved into the den where he lay on the futon and I sat on the floor and watched a movie about a criminal on the run who befriends a boy who's a Jehovah's Witness and has never had a Halloween costume. It was a movie about trust and about the relativity of crime, and finally it was about living a worthwhile life before it's too late. It didn't look good now that the cops were chasing them. Sam had seen this before and wandered into the kitchen. I heard him open the refrigerator, one of the comforts of home.

I called out, 'I don't want to see this ending.'

Sam re-entered the room. 'Can't they see he's trying to give that kid something? People in authority need to understand what's really happening. It's like with Steele. Just when he's in trouble, the Vets Administration cut his benefits.'

'What happened?'

'He's gone downhill. Hell, it can be a long winter here. He got caught driving under the influence, had a warning from the VA and felt bad. Then there was this woman. When she wiggled her fingers at him, he ended up fixing her roof. He bought all the materials and she never paid him a cent. He was chasing her in bars as far as Garrison. Another DWI. Now he's lost his license for a year and is down to minimum benefits.'

'Did they offer any counseling?'

'Not that I know of.'

'Why didn't he drink at the Red Eye and then walk home?'

Sam snorted. 'Haven't you been listening? There was a woman involved.'

The truck was an adventure. My brother loaned me a flashlight that worked if you held it in a certain way and showed me the side light, then took his pillow back into the house. The truck smelled of boy, and showers at truck stops, and loneliness that is controlled to the point of contentment. I rolled my jean jacket into a tube and wriggled into his sleeping bag, and left the door of the truck open because I loved the lake air and the rustling of the trees and the way my muscles had relaxed from the swimming and the certainty that I would sleep well.

Except the Kevin Costner movie bothered me: it's so easy to have your actions misinterpreted, so easy to lose direction and convince yourself that it's okay to drive when you've had a few drinks and live in the middle of nowhere.

I was thinking about Steele and how I'd seen him at the Red Eye last year. I had a lot of respect for these old resorts that reinvented themselves to keep going. It was a corny afternoon with an accordion player for the older crowd and two-dollar tacos and a table of widows in the corner gambling, pulling pull tabs the way I eat popcorn, one kernel after another as fast as I can, which really makes you thirsty, makes you order another drink — and my brother and Steele at the bar with an empty stool between them, watching pre-season football on the screen in the corner. I was thinking how much I resented the onset of football when it was still summer, but I'd sat down and ordered a screwdriver anyway.

Sam said, 'Steele, you remember my sister Cynthia, don't you?' And Steele had looked at me with his unreadable eyes and sort of grinned and asked how long I was visiting and I told him a week. 'That's nice,' he answered, 'must be peaceful for you.' He looked back at the television and halfway through my drink, I thought: Why am I sitting here on this beautiful afternoon? And I walked out.

Things had been going okay for him, it seemed to me: he'd looked good. Now his pump was broken and he couldn't drive. I fell asleep wondering what Joe Steele was doing right now, but I knew really. He was in his cabin with his dog sipping a quart of Mickey's cheap and powerful malt liquor.

The next day, when I came back from swimming, Sam and Jerry were sitting at Sam's picnic table, drinking. The lawn was half-mown and the lawnmower was lying on its side with a tool box nearby. They each had a bottle of beer and Kahlúa in the shot glasses I'd given Sam once for his birthday. It was just like him to have a cocktail party and not invite me.

Sam was telling a trucker story about a middle-aged couple who'd been sailing for ten months when they'd decided to go home. They'd found Sam on his website that he was so proud of, and hired him to drive their boat back east.

Jerry nodded hello at me so as not to interrupt. I had an ancient black towel tied around my waist and I caught him taking a quick look at my legs. I didn't know if I was a good sister, but I was a good listener and so we heard about the huge fight the couple had on their flight home and, by the time Sam arrived in Vermont with the boat, somebody had filed for divorce. When Sam stopped by the house for his check, the wife invited him out to dinner.

He looked at us and laughed: that's all we were getting.

'So,' Sam said, 'my sister's just swum around The Point. It's a ritual.'

I reached for his glass and sipped. 'I saw an eagle.'

'Where did you launch?' Jerry asked, and I smiled at him. Only a man would get a woman mixed up with a boat.

'At Gail's. She lets everybody use her beach.'

Jerry nodded. 'So you're a good swimmer?'

'It's not that far around The Point,' my brother said.

I laughed. 'What were you two up to before this party started?'

'Jerry did a water run for Steele, then we decided to cut his grass, but he doesn't want our help today. Not a good day, I guess.'

'He doesn't want us touching his boat either so we can't sneak some gas into his tank. When he can't take his dog fishing, he gets down.'

I asked, 'Doesn't he also own a rowboat?'

'Sold it,' Sam said.

Jerry was studying the label on his beer bottle. 'They're hungry, him and Queenie. Last night they turned up while I was grilling hamburgers. When I offered, Steele declined, but Queenie's eyes told the story. I grilled that dog a burger and put it in a bun on a plate.'

We were all quiet, picturing the dog wolfing that dinner. I wondered if pride was a habit or an addiction or a ritual.

'It'll be okay,' Sam announced. 'He's going inside in September and it'll do him good: three square meals a day and on the wagon. His benefits will go back up and he'll be two months closer to having his license back.'

I looked at Sam: he hadn't told me that part of the story. Anyway, September was more than a week away.

'They call it rehabilitation,' Jerry said, 'but those mattresses are only five inches thick and hard as shit. Don't make sense how depriving a man of a good night's rest is going to help.' And the way he said it made me wonder if he'd been there and done it.

'Well,' he drawled, 'guess I'll be keeping an eye on both your places this fall. It'll give me something to do besides shoot deer.'

With that he gave us a little salute and left. All I knew was that a few years ago Jerry had a girlfriend until he'd tried to shoot the lock off her front door. Nobody pressed charges, Sam had assured me, because nobody got hurt. And he'd shrugged it off. Like now. It was unsettling, the casual way Sam and Jerry had appraised Steele's current situation and decided to leave it alone. It didn't make sense to me the same way it didn't make sense to Sam how the VA had given Steele maximum benefits when he first came back so he didn't have to work. Because he'd wanted to, Sam told me, he was motivated. Because you wouldn't want too much time alone.

I started clearing the empties off the table and then I stopped: this wasn't my mess.

That night Sam concocted his super-duper Barbie doll sauce and we grilled steaks outside. I made a salad and opened the bottle of red. And so we sat across from each other at the picnic table and toasted the lake.

We tasted the wine and the meat.

'Sam, why couldn't you look at Steele's boat today?'

'He's not communicating. Maybe try tomorrow.'

I thought how tomorrow was our last full day here, then we'd be driving down to the Cities for the State Fair. We didn't make it every year, but this year we would.

'Sam, what would you have done if your lottery number had come up?'

He took a slug of wine. 'I don't know. We were different people then.'

'You must have thought about it.'

'Ya, and I sure couldn't see myself on the front line. Not like Steele. Tunnel rats. His kind took the brunt.'

'Do you feel at all guilty?'

Did he hesitate while he helped himself to salad?

'Women are susceptible to guilt.'

I ignored that. 'It was a long time ago but we've lived with the ripples. PTSD and suicides. Men who obeyed orders and when they came back, they weren't really here.'

Sam had been looking down at his plate, but now he threw me a look. 'No one is going to starve. No one is dying of neglect. And how these guys live is none of your business. If you have water, you can last for a month.'

At that moment, I hated his logic.

We ate in silence until he stood up from the table, saying, 'It's my turn for the bike.'

He might as well have said, *Don't wait up.*

I had pushed my luck and was in danger of outstaying my welcome. Sam needed his space and was doing his best. I soaked the dishes in the sink and went outside and saw the boundary stake that had been bent by the bulldozer when he'd started clearing his land. How proud he'd been when the ground was level and it looked possible for something else to emerge. He'd parked his old silver trailer there for years while he saved money. Six years ago, when he'd given me a ride from the Cities, I'd fallen asleep in the traffic and he'd tapped me on the head with new, rolled-up architectural drawings of his house and drawled: 'The future is now.'

And that night I'd splurged on a bottle of cheap champagne. 'Sam, this is for you. The future is now.'

'*Mi casa, su casa,*' he'd answered and raised his glass to mine.

It was the closest I'd ever heard him come to telling me that I was always welcome. Mediocre champagne and a fine memory, all rolled into one. Now I shivered; the heat of the day didn't stay around as long. Summer would soon be over.

I walked Bachelors Road to Gail's beach as slowly as I

could. At Jerry's there was one light on in the trailer and a string of lit-up stars on the front window that would look even better when it was dark.

I sat on the bench at the end of Gail's dock. I was wishing for more red wine, but made do with cloud formations and the lapping sound on those slippery stones that were a killer on bare feet when you walked out; so much easier to slide on your belly. I wanted to swim, but it would be cold now so I wrestled with that. Wrestled with the idea of walking past Steele's to the Red Eye. And I had time to think about last summer when the Doors music blasted out of Steele's cabin, old music from the Vietnam War era. Then I thought of Steele driving to Garrison, going into a bar with torn plastic on the stools and a calendar by the cash register with last month on it because no one had bothered to turn it over. I pictured him needing to ask about that woman, but embarrassed, and I wondered if Steele had kept going into those tunnels to look for Viet Cong and their ammunition because it was too embarrassing not to.

I was camped out in the den when Sam came back. I'd taken the red towel off the top of the lamp so I could read and, when he came in, he replaced it, but nicely. He let me stay on the futon while he filled the sink with clean water. I'd left the glasses for him. When I heard the other TV go on, I tried not to take it personally.

He called out, 'I'm going to town tomorrow if you want some diversion. Taking the truck through the car wash.'

And that was how we made a plan for the last day. It wasn't late when I said goodnight. I took the flashlight and his jacket to throw on top of the sleeping bag and fell asleep with the breeze a little cooler on my face. When an animal in the woods cried out, I woke up: two howls or one long one? It was loud and near and it happened once more and then I jumped when Sam opened the screen door of the truck.

'Cynthia, you all right?'

I mumbled something.

'This place can be wild. You don't have any food in here?'

I shook my head even though he couldn't see me.

Then, 'Lock this door tonight.'

And I was by myself again, but not afraid really. Just alert and humbled.

As usual, Sam slept late and I took full advantage, doing what I love: walking down to Angel's Pond to visit the family of ducks and see the water lilies. The fact that I wouldn't be back here for a year made me go down the ladder a little quicker and swim out further.

When I got back to the house, Sam's door was still firmly closed so I grabbed a cinnamon roll and the bike and rode off to check out the waves on the other side of The Point, but I ended up at Steele's crossroad. I was a little high with the morning and hunger and the silence and that tantalizing feeling of time slipping away, slipping.

I stopped and looked at his cabin. The shrubs in front of the windows needed trimming and ferns were growing through the front steps.

Sam wanted a shiny truck so he could make a good impression on the firm who were going to fix his generator. At the car wash, we stayed in the truck while water whooshed around us.

I aimed my camera at his profile. 'This will make a good picture.'

Sam lounged behind the steering wheel. 'So wait for the colored wax. It reminds me of the rainbow ice cream cones at the Fair, remember them? You can still buy them.'

When the wax appeared running down the windows – pink, blue and yellow – I burst out laughing. 'Sam, but blue is wrong. It should be green. They don't have blue ice cream.'

'Want to bet? Twenty bucks. We can check it out tomorrow. I'm making you nervous now, aren't I? Not so sure of yourself, and I like it that way.'

Then we had lunch at The Bakery, the place with fresh fish and delicious bread where Sam picked up the local paper as we entered and I chose the table by the window so I could see the post office across from the dentist's office. Sam told me he'd been to see the new dentist, a good-looking redhead whom he had trouble looking in the eye, and I said she probably liked it that way.

When we drove back, Sam took the road past Steele's.

'Who's going to take care of Queenie?' was all that I said, but Sam glared at me.

'Leave it alone, Cynthia.' And then he said, 'The guys might go fishing later. I could take you out now for a boat ride so you're not left out.'

And I thought about how many things there were to do here and I hadn't done them. The croquet set was still in the garage. I hadn't dangled my feet in the lake, eating a bag of monkey nuts, shells floating in the water like little canoes. We hadn't lit any fireworks. I said, 'I'd love a boat ride. Then you go fishing. I'll be fine.'

I carried the brown paper bag down to Steele's. It felt like walking from the grocery store to the car. The storm door was pulled shut but not locked.

What had I expected? Bed made, the dishes were washed. There was a six pack of empties on the kitchen counter and a dirty frying pan on the stove, a patina of flavors, though he'd use another word.

The shades were pulled down at the front and in the bathroom — old-fashioned khaki ones fragile to the touch: I hadn't seen those in years.

I put the bag of leftovers in the refrigerator. I wanted to sit in his chair and look at his bookshelf. I wanted to learn something. Going into the bedroom would be overstepping the mark. I didn't want to start something I couldn't finish.

There was a carton of cigarettes on the table and I felt sorry for him then, momentarily. We all have addictions but tobacco is such a tacky one, and then I remembered what Sam had told me he'd learned from the Bachelors: in prison they don't give you matches so you have to take your radio apart and flick two wires together to create a spark. When one guy smokes, a dozen smoke. 'Chain smokers', I'd joked. Then I pictured buckets of water being passed along man-to-man, fighting a fire. Or ending up on Steele's doorstep. Another way to save a life.

I swam one more time and the moon was not full and you couldn't call the water luminous but it was calm and warm and all the years disappeared. Sam and I were still at home where everything was more or less whole because our father had come back from a war he believed in to make money and prosper. And Steele and Jerry and Dwayne were kids growing up in other Midwest

13

neighborhoods while the American dream was going up the flagpole and we all pledged allegiance to the flag because our hearts had not been chipped away at yet.

Sam and I locked up his house and climbed into his truck to get on the road as early as possible, find a parking space, ring our friends and stroll toward our meeting point at the beer garden to sit out the hottest part of the day. We had tickets for an old rock and roll group, half of whom had survived a plane crash. You had to hand it to them, Sam said; either they loved their tradition or they couldn't find a new way to live. We didn't care. We were going to sit in the grandstand and watch the fine spectacle.

Two days later I flew home.

Sam had his generator repaired and then went on the road to pay for it. The next time I spoke to him, he had another story for me: about a Russian man in polyester trousers, sitting at a desk in the middle of an empty warehouse in Missouri.

Steele went inside and gained fifteen pounds and dried out and almost quit smoking.

We all dried out that autumn, we all took stock.

DANCING ON THE DOCK, 2008

It was Raoul who pointed out Edie's posture – when he put his hand against her shoulder and walked her gently two steps back to the kitchen wall and said, 'Some yoga and you will move better.'

'I thought I moved all right,' she answered, and when he laughed she recognized how she liked the low bubble of that sound.

He showed her the space between her lower back and the wall: he could slip his hand into it. It was because her shoulder blades stuck out too far.

'Do you feel these shoulder blades? These are winged scapulas. Nothing seriously wrong, but your upper body is a little weak, Edie. When you take a walk, you could carry cans of Spam and lift them up and down for your core muscles.'

She looked at him.

Raoul said, 'Don't worry. There's no damage to your *serratus anterior* that I can feel. Walking is good for you. And your bike is good for people your age.'

And he sounded like the young Mexican doctor he was: he'd changed right before her eyes and, in the early summer light of June, she started preparing herself. He would go soon and he'd probably not ever be back this way and that would be the end of it.

He'd put her spare room to good use. The loft with the low slanted roof and one window facing the street. It was just a double mattress on the floor and a dresser, a clothes rail and a rug, and on the far side one built-in cupboard which of course Edie had filled with junk when she moved in four years ago.

She could remember the day he'd answered her advert on the bulletin board of the Co-op where she worked. He was traveling through Minnesota, on his way to the famous Mayo Clinic to take up a residency, and he was taking his time. He liked to explore the small towns, he told her, so different from Mexico, and her town of Cambridge and the Co-op, with its bookshop attached to the food store, lured him in.

It had been her day off, the day he phoned, and she'd gone to meet him on her bicycle.

'I am resting for two months before working,' he'd said. 'I would like to see your little room please.' And there he was outside the Co-op, sprawled on a chair in front of the bookshop reading, a mug in front of him next to a huge sandwich with organic sprouts seeping out the edges.

He looked taller than he was and handsome enough with those beautiful teeth. And she noticed that it took him a long time to eat his lunch, chewing thoughtfully and asking questions.

'You eat so slow,' she said.

'Americanos inhale their food; it is poor for the

digestion.'

When she asked what the notebook was for, he said it was his travel diary, impressions of all the places he'd seen so far. And she asked if he'd been to Austin, the town in this state where Spam was invented, and ended up laughing, explaining what Spam was.

'I have to tell you,' she said, 'that the café on Main Street serves it for breakfast on the first Saturday of every month. And if your name is Sam, your breakfast is free because they put a sign on your table: Sam sat here on Spam Sat.'

'Where am I?' He had thrown up his hands in wonder. 'I am in the undiscovered heart of America.'

And that cinched the deal; yes, he could move in.

He had brought his coffee grinder and put it on the counter next to her old-fashioned olive-green stove from the '80s which had come with the house. She liked the smell of Mexican coffee in the kitchen, his shaving things in the bathroom. He liked the room at the top of the stairs in her home that needed some work on slightly run-down Tacoma Avenue.

So they'd settled into a routine. Coffee grinder in the morning, clank of the hot water heater last thing at night.

She'd never really liked living here by herself, so now the house felt warmer and she made an extra effort to put things away. Having another person around was like drawing around your furniture, your house, your job with a thick felt-tip pen, everything more clearly defined.

'You like your job,' he'd reassured her once when she'd been complaining about it.

She did. She could handle being a manager because she shared it with two others. She liked her four-day week and she liked the bookstore, which hosted occasional readings and book signings. She'd gladly paid her Co-op membership fee when she'd moved there and then a year ago she'd invested in a 'member loan' because it made her feel part of something and she liked receiving a dividend check at the beginning of March – a treat, just when you thought you couldn't stand one more minute of winter.

He'd smiled at that.

Two months was going fast.

And then one June night they sat at the kitchen table longer than usual, and it was warm enough for her to kick her shoes off and feel the warmth of the linoleum. They had eaten slowly his wonderful bean and cheese 'hotdish' – he'd adopted the Midwestern word for it – which he'd baked in 'The Cadillac' – his joke of a name for her stove.

They talked about the book signing that afternoon, the young woman reading stories about her grandmother near the Rum River, and he'd bought the book and sat at the table and read a story to Edie and she loved it; she didn't want him to stop.

He read the last satisfying paragraph, giving it its due, and now it was finished so he closed the book, touching the Manila paper, running his forefinger down the green and gold front cover, watching her.

'You could write your stories,' he said.

The spell was over. She reached for his dirty plate and scraped her chair back.

'No, I couldn't.'

'You've told me a few interesting ones. You and Jerry running away to North Dakota.'

She made a face; had she told him all that? How they'd eloped before Jerry was drafted and she still had the photos and an old tablecloth hidden in her brown plastic suitcase; how he'd come back from Vietnam wounded, shot in the arm; and then how long it had taken to get pregnant with Michael.

Raoul was watching her now walk over to the sink.

'You have to stand up for yourself,' he said.

'What?'

'I mean, stand up straighter.' That's when he backed her up to the wall to show her her shoulder blades. 'Your posture says something about you.'

'Like what?'

'You do not look as tall as you are, Edie.'

'And on a good day you look taller than you really are,' she answered.

He laughed. 'So I'm told. Thank you. But what is holding you back? You live here by yourself. You are not married but you are not divorced. Are you hiding? Maybe you have more to say to him. I don't know. You can think about it this summer while I am memorizing articles from medical journals.'

She put the dishes in the dishwasher while he went outside and looked at the sky, which he often did before he went to sleep. Sometimes he took a walk around the block. Sometimes in the middle of the day he took off in his car and stayed away the night. She knew his habits and she realized that she would miss them more than she'd admitted, but it wasn't really a crush, was it? After all, she was almost sixty and he was twenty years younger. It wasn't really a friendship. It was just the way things were.

The next week she drove up to Cross Lake straight after work, north on Highway 65. She had the radio turned on low but wasn't really listening. She was conscious of sitting up straight in the car, aware of her shoulder blades and letting them settle, aware of summer coming toward her. There was something about Raoul leaving in ten days that gave her the urgency, made her think about time and prodded her into moving. She wondered if she could find where Jerry lived on The Point.

And then she remembered the first time he'd ever taken her up there — it was '68, the end of deer-hunting season and he wanted to show her where they'd gone. He'd only been back from Vietnam five weeks and it didn't sound like a good idea to her to go hunting, but his cousin Zac had already paid for a cabin at a resort. So Edie May, the young wife, had gone along with it, in spite of the facts that she didn't want her husband out of her sight, that she hadn't had enough of him since he'd come back, and she was still worried about his left arm where he'd been shot below the elbow, though she only had half the story of how it happened.

'I want you to see the lake,' he'd said and so they'd driven up in the middle of the week when the resort was dead quiet, where the massive waves on the big lake were not comforting. And he'd taken her to the deer stand in the woods where he and Zac had waited for their shot: the stand had a ladder and looked like a tree house.

Then she'd asked if they could drive around the lake, and they'd watched two men in green rubber waders dismantling an aluminum dock for the winter and Jerry had told her how most of the docks were still wood because things weren't too modernized up there yet, and he'd driven slowly, just looking, connecting with forces that she couldn't see.

They'd stopped in a café for lunch and she'd watched him cut into a hot turkey sandwich with his fork and she'd worried that he avoided using his left hand when he could get away with it.

And when they got home, he'd more or less thrown her down on the bed and unzipped her jeans and she'd watched him not look at her and that's when she'd decided he was not the same man and didn't know what to do about it.

Now, driving in the direction of the lake, she put that memory together with what Raoul had said to her that night in her kitchen, and it was as if the evening light gave her clarity and, as she pressed her foot down on the accelerator, she wondered if she'd left herself behind somewhere.

Now Edie May watched out for signs for the lake and the towns on both sides of it, Garrison and Wahkon, and knew enough to stay near the east side until she saw a sign for Angel's Pond.

She followed it. She had been here last year when Jerry was planning to drive to Florida to see Michael, and she'd delivered a care package for their son – a pale lemon polo shirt and an airtight package of his favorite chocolate chip brownies. She'd felt sentimental about the old days so she'd also handed Jerry some brownies for himself. 'I don't want these in the freezer,' she'd explained. 'I'll just eat them.' And he'd thanked her with the puzzled politeness used between people who no longer know each other well.

Could she find him now?

She remembered a road with two different turnings, one to an old resort further down past a boat harbor called Angel's Pond and the other took you by big golden log cabins before you found the dirt road and the row of trailers where Jerry lived. Bachelors Road, he'd called it for a joke, but sure enough one of them had nailed a hand-painted sign to the tree.

But tonight she only drove as far as the first log cabin

and, in the dusky light, she walked down to the lake and out onto a dock which was old wood and smooth to her hand when she touched it.

It was a lake you either loved because it was so big or hated because it was too big. It looked cold and lonely to her tonight, in spite of remembering how Michael had told her about taking a boat ride around The Point, how it took most of an hour if the wind was against you, how the jut of land shielded you on one side or the other. She'd seen it in his eyes: he loved this lake like Jerry did and she'd consoled herself by hoping Cross Lake would be enough to keep Michael in Minnesota, but it wasn't. Two years ago her son had come home from Iraq, just to leave her again for Florida.

There was a bench placed at the end of the dock facing out. She must have sat there for a long time while her eyes adjusted and then she could make out lights on the watery horizon.

When she walked back to her car she looked up the road to see which trailer was Jerry's. In the dusk she saw the one with blue lights around the window that faced the lake; did she remember those lights? His driveway was empty.

The day Raoul left for Rochester was a warm one and when Edie May walked through her front door then into the kitchen, and saw the fifty-dollar bills fanned out on the table, she said out loud, 'Love is shit.'

And then she turned on the faucet and ran the water cold and colder, and drank two glasses because one thing she had taught herself was that sometimes when she thought she was hungry, she was really thirsty. Well, she was thirsty now. Shriveling up.

It wasn't like she hadn't known he was going. It was always a two-month arrangement. But then he'd asked to stay an extra three days which slid into four and it had unbalanced her somehow until he kissed her goodbye.

Last night he'd cleaned out the old charcoal broiler and they'd sipped beer on the back step for a long time before bringing their plates inside.

He'd surprised her by pulling a harmonica out of his pocket, and she'd danced around the kitchen for a few glorious minutes in her bare feet and then he'd said he was going to walk around the neighborhood, and she'd said that she wasn't going to bother with the dishes, she was going to take a bath. Then he kissed her half on the mouth and half on her cheek and when she got out of the tub and went into her bedroom she was pretty sure he wasn't back yet and, in spite of herself, she turned away from her closed door with the crack of light around it, and fell asleep.

Now her three words hung in the air as she looked around the kitchen.

It wasn't as if he'd taken anything away from her. He'd loaded the dishwasher and left the empty bottles tucked in their carrier by the door. But of course that's not really what she meant.

In the evening light she walked through the house. She forced herself to look in the bathroom, look at where his books had gone from the coffee table. She stood at the bottom of the stairs and missed all the things he'd left there: reading glasses and coffee cups, his medical journals and his *Time* magazines, and she knew that the resentment she felt was loneliness.

The summer felt long and tangled in front of her. And Raoul's words last night were on her mind: 'You keep talking about running away, do you know that?' And she'd stared at him, neither encouraging nor discouraging him from continuing so he'd said, 'Count them. You both ran away to get married and then Jerry ran away from Vietnam, and now Michael's run to Everglades City.'

'Edie,' he said to get her attention because she'd turned away. 'We all do it. Look at me, I've run away to Minnesota. Left someone behind. I hope she doesn't wait for me.' And so she'd tried to be the kind of listener that he was: undistracted and open, and she learned about his married cousin and how he'd kept studying to keep away from her.

'It's life,' he'd shrugged. 'Maybe we can do some things about it. Maybe not. It's your own decision how far you want to understand.'

And then he'd asked her why she didn't use her real name, the one she signed her marriage certificate with and she'd said, 'I never liked it. Edith. It's a grown-up name. It's not very beautiful.'

'You are saved from being beautiful with your long face like a horse. It's better, in my estimation.'

And she'd laughed hard and shaken her head, but that didn't mean that she hadn't heard the compliment and tucked it away.

Edie worked her days at the Co-op, watering vegetables with the mini-sprinkling system and grinding coffee beans so the smell permeated the store. She bought a Jane Fonda yoga DVD and brought the mirror down from upstairs so she could watch herself master Downward-Facing Dog, which was harder than it looked.

The day she took the loft room apart and cleaned it was the same day she went through her desk and looked for her divorce file. She washed the sheets and the mattress pad and when she rolled the rug up to sweep, she found two twenty-dollar bills. She'd only just recovered from the fan of fifties he'd left the last morning, so she thought that this was either his emergency fund or it was a gift, gas money to use when she visited him, and they'd laugh about it when he got in touch.

It was a nice thought and she laughed at herself now. But she liked the feel of the old floorboards and remembered the dock up at Cross Lake and she knew that dancing around the kitchen wasn't really enough. She wished for wood under her feet. Well, the living room floor was stripped boards – a nasty blue from when she'd moved in and tried staining it and it came out the color of an angry sky, and so she'd covered it up with a cheap carpet.

She went downstairs to take a look at it now and rolled it back from the front door and it made the room look bigger, big enough for a party.

Edie invited twelve people over on Thursday night, a nibble and a dribble before the weekend, and she borrowed CDs from Sandra, the younger woman who cut her hair, and Edie stashed beer and wine in the refrigerator and made vegetable dips. She felt relieved when cars pulled into her driveway and Sandra and her boyfriend turned up on bicycles and Edie lit the candles in turquoise holders all the way up the stairs.

She'd made her older sister Rebecca promise to come because Rebecca was a good sport, and sociable. It took the heaviness out of it, dancing while it was still light, with the front and back doors open, a few people singing along to the Beach Boys.

At nine o'clock Edie brought each guest a paper plate with potato salad next to a Sloppy Joe, and she turned the music down and everyone sat where they could, they were all hungry. Sandra's boyfriend, Andy, ate standing up in the doorway. Then Andy asked if she had any decaf and, when he followed her into the kitchen, his eyes slid over her in a way that reminded Edie of meeting Tony at the bowling alley last January, when Sandra had talked her into joining that Winter League.

Edie'd had a little fling, staying over at Tony's house twice but then not calling him back, and now when she smiled at Andy, it occurred to her that there was something wrong with not responding, or not really caring about someone else's responses, not even the day she saw Tony in front of the hardware store with the woman in the red hat.

The coffee tasted good with the chocolate chip brownies she passed around and that seemed to be the signal for everyone to go home.

Rebecca, who was in the kitchen dumping paper plates into the waste paper basket, called out, 'Well, that went all right.'

'I can be around people.'

'Who said you couldn't?' Rebecca had walked into the living room now. 'Why are you standing like that? You look like you're about to take off.'

'It's my posture. My shoulder blades stick out.'

'Who told you that?'

'Raoul.'

'Your Mexican doctor? Listen, Edie, you need to go out more.'

'I want to dance this summer. Now how the hell am I going to do that?'

'God, you sound old. Find a boyfriend. It can't be that hard.'

And in the night Edie woke up when she heard a floorboard creak upstairs and for a minute felt elated until she realized that it was her sister.

A few days later in the bookshop she stopped to look at the greeting cards.

In the Cryptic Humor section, she picked up one that said: 'Okay, so you're too old for a mid-life crisis. . . but what about a midnight crisis?' With a cartoon woman with sticking-out hair, holding a spoon in one hand and a giant ice cream carton in the other, and a clock in the background striking twelve. And inside – in bold print: 'When you're finished indulging, review your goals and make a hair appointment.'

Edie read the card again.

That was the night she drove back up to Cross Lake and parked outside the first log cabin. So quiet during the week – where was everyone? She walked to the end of the dock again, took off her sandals and dangled her feet in the water; it would be perfectly dark soon and it felt right to look across the lake and see hardly any lights. Hardly any boats. Room to think.

God knows she'd been drifting long enough, though she'd never really thought about it like that before. But what did she want? The water felt cold and dangerous.

She wanted to dance on all the docks around the lake. And she needed a divorce.

The lawyer's secretary said, 'That was three years ago. You better make an appointment.'

And when she was sitting in front of the lawyer, he asked, 'Are you sure you want this divorce to go ahead?'

And she said, 'He's been living in a trailer for nearly four years. Most men leave for another woman, but Jerry left me for a lake.'

The lawyer smiled and turned to reach for the file. 'Have you talked to your husband about this? I mean recently.'

Edie shook her head.

'Well, do you and Jerry have financial matters to settle?'

'He already made me sell the house; that was the big thing.'

The lawyer looked at her. 'I doubt that he made you do anything. In my opinion, if you want this to go smoothly, don't blame it all on him. And you might want to tell your son before Jerry does.'

It made her think.

Two days later she phoned Ted's Old Fishing Shop in Everglades City, and listened to her son's voice on the answering machine: 'Hi, we've gone fishing. If you want to rent a boat or hire a guide, try this cell number and, when I'm in reach, I'll be glad to do business.'

And it made her happy and sad to hear his voice, well-adjusted and confident.

'Come on,' Jerry had said to her when Michael announced his plan to move to Everglades City. 'Give the kid a break. He'll be close to nature.'

'There's plenty of nature in Minnesota.'

'Sometimes you need to start over.'

Edie, sitting in her living room with the telephone receiver in her hand, remembering how those words had hurt because by then Jerry had been gone for two years and was this his idea of an explanation? And after she'd stalled on the house sale, then finally bought her own place in Cambridge, she made sure she still had room for Michael when he returned from active duty. They could have remodeled the loft together. Maybe Jerry would have driven down once in a while to see them and they could have been a family.

Instead, here she was, hesitating before she dialed the cell phone number because her son would ask what he always asked: 'When are you coming to visit, Mom? Come on, you got nothing better to do.'

Which didn't strike her as funny any longer. It was too near the truth. She'd never had much to do after he left home, never pushed herself to find a direction. She'd drifted from her father's house into Jerry's house and the reason she didn't want to visit Michael's house was because she didn't want to see him happy and settled without her.

Edie was figuring a few things out.

One night she ended up at the secluded boat harbor, Angel's Pond. 'PRIVATE BOAT HARBOR', the sign read, with rules listed underneath. Three boats covered up with tarps were rocking very slightly. Four docks empty. Some water lilies that she couldn't see very clearly. And a picnic table with a sign that read: 'No lifeguard, swim at your own risk'.

Dance at your own risk, she thought.

She danced by herself on the dock nearest the picnic table.

Near the opening to the lake was a pedal boat and she sat in it for a while and listened. The more she listened, the more she heard. Water moving. A fish jumped. And something moaned from a place over the trees near the houses on the dead-end circle.

She had parked near the small green house and she walked back there now. It didn't look like anyone was home but they all seemed to leave lights on. Then she walked back to Jerry's trailer where the blue stars around the front window reminded her how his eyes could be blue and cold, or they could twinkle.

She knew the door wouldn't be locked, and she knocked once.

'Jerry,' she said softly.

She could make out the table underneath the side window, an armchair, and his bed in the corner. She felt him watching her body in the non-light, lithe and straight.

'Edie?' He sighed and sat up.

She waited for him to ask what the hell she thought she was doing, but it stayed quiet.

'Jerry, remember the first time you saw a dead body? I know it was in Nam, but you never wanted to talk about it, never even told me about that accident when you got shot, but I've been thinking about how my dad and I went to the public beach one suppertime and there was a body, all blue, on the sand. People stood around until the ambulance came, and my dad said to me: *So there you have it, Edie.*'

Edie waited to make sure Jerry was listening.

'I guess that's the first time I knew life wasn't going to be perfect. Maybe it's why I like water but I don't love it. I didn't even go swimming last year. I wouldn't want to live up here.'

Edie looked around, appraising something. 'But what I want to ask is when did you know about our marriage? When did you see something dead?'

'You're being dramatic. It's never just one thing.'

30

She shook her head. 'No, Jerry. You stopped talking.'

'If I did, I stopped talking to everybody.'

'That's my point. You have to talk to your wife.'

'It's too late to write the rules.'

'You're right.' She shivered. 'But it was better for a long time when Michael was born. We both know that.'

'Christ, what are you doing?' And then, more kindly: 'Listen, Edie, this isn't a good idea, going over all this.'

And she remembered how he used to lower his voice and that made his words important, just for her.

'Do you have a girlfriend, Jerry?'

'She doesn't like it here. I stay at her place sometimes.'

She took a good look at the bed, somewhere between a single and a double, and at his silhouette, his hand touching his mustache.

He asked, 'You feeling sorry for yourself now?'

'No, it's not that simple, it's never just one thing, is it? You should lock your door, Jerry. It's sort of wild up here.'

She walked fast to her car. Her shoulders were cold and she was glad for the sweater on the front seat. She thought she saw another light go on in the green house, so she didn't turn on her engine, she just sat there letting the past come into her.

She'd been right about when Michael was born: Jerry couldn't stop talking about his beautiful boy and how they were a real family, even if it had taken them so long to have a baby.

Those were good years, nearly normal years. She'd gotten used to Jerry's silences and his out-of-the-blue outbursts and if her husband didn't really talk to her much, her son always did, even as a kid. Then suddenly Michael was grown-up, living on his own but phoning and finding reasons to come by. Michael, standing in front of the refrigerator, drinking orange juice and telling her about the war in Iraq, and the news program he'd watched and how this wasn't going to end any time soon – and she'd asked him when he planned to tell his father that he was enlisting and he'd replied, 'Soon.'

And a week later in the car on the way to Michael's apartment, Jerry had glanced sideways at her, the beginning of a sneer on his face. 'You know about this, don't you?'

And that was the first nail in the coffin, and the second was Jerry standing in Michael's parking lot, leaning against his old black Buick, sucking a toothpick, and their son walking toward them in the moccasins they'd given him for Christmas: 'You want to talk about this, Dad?'

And Jerry had answered: 'I want you to say you've thought this over.'

'Been sleeping with it for a month. You had your war. This one's mine.'

It was as if Jerry couldn't stop himself; his arm came up at the same time the sneer came onto his face and he hit his son hard in the stomach.

Everything stopped for a few seconds while all three of them reasoned out their separate thoughts. She touched her son's arm.

'It's okay, Ma. I been training.'

He was staring down at his stomach, like he could imagine the muscle and sinew, as if considering how much force the skin could take before breaking. As she watched her son step back from them, clenching and unclenching his fist, calculating his best move forward, Edie knew that his chances of survival were as good as they could be. He did not have his father's anger, and she hoped to God that he wouldn't come home with it.

Now Edie May sat still in her car and thought it over. Jerry did know what war was like and Michael didn't want to listen, so Jerry felt dismissed. He was just trying to save his son's life. She could see her husband's side of it more clearly than she ever had, but that didn't mean that she forgave him. He didn't want Michael to go through what he had, what he was still going through: nights when he didn't sleep; mornings when he'd walked out of work at eleven o'clock and called it early lunch; afternoons by himself, fishing on some lake. And her drifting through those days, without much to show for it when he came home, and how she didn't want to see it in his eyes that she was lazy and should try harder.

'You all run away,' Raoul had said. And she'd made a face because she felt stuck, sedentary, slow at figuring out patterns; it didn't really add up until now. The way she'd drifted into a life with Jerry and then he'd drifted away. The day he walked in the door and said, 'I'm moving up to Cross Lake. On the east side, there are plots of land going really cheap.'

There'd been some sort of scandal between an old married guy and his gray-haired girlfriend and their trailers were up for sale. Jerry had grinned at this point: 'Marriages don't seem to survive up there. I'm gonna re-name it Bachelors Road.'

That comment had hurt, like their marriage didn't count, had never counted very much, so she'd raised her voice, 'I'm willing to work on this, but you go hide in the woods like an animal if you have to.'

Jerry had thrown back: 'Work on what?' And then, more softly: 'I don't want to be here when the phone rings with news about Michael. You can have your divorce and we'll talk about money later, but I'm going up there tomorrow, and maybe I'll sign something.'

Well, there were a lot of nails in that coffin. Edie rubbed her eyes and turned on the motor. It was exhausting looking at the past; that was a good reason not to do it.

The summer of 2008 was the summer that Edie worked most of this out and came to terms with some of it. She stopped thinking in that tiny little place in her brain that Raoul would send her a card or an invitation. She stopped thinking that the divorce would happen miraculously without actually talking to Jerry. She stopped thinking that Michael would move back from Everglades City next month. She made an effort to be friendlier, not so remote. When Sandra said, 'Let's get together and go to an estate sale,' Edie picked up the newspaper and pinned her down. When Rebecca said, 'Will you take care of my dogs so I can go on a date and maybe not come home for three days?', Edie laughed and then brought over homemade tomato sauce and extra spaghetti because her sister might not have enough.

Did she feel better? She felt fine. Fine was a good word, good and vague. Work was fine. Her life was just fine. You don't die of loneliness, she told herself once in the middle of the night, and then turned over and went back to sleep.

Because she would have liked company driving around the lake, scanning from the road for the docks, trying to look like she knew where she was going, like she belonged and, in the dark, taking her sandals off and risking splinters to dance.

There was one night when a back door light came on and a young man in jeans and flip flops came out of a cabin. 'Who's there?'

And she froze momentarily before replying, 'Sorry, wrong dock. Thought I left something out here.' Which she'd practiced and hoped she'd never have to use. Which made her a little meeker, and she'd gone back to Angel's Pond which felt like her own territory now, and danced for a long time at the first golden cabin because she'd figured out that their boat suspended from the side of the dock meant they were weekenders and not there.

And there was another night when Edie realized that her August wedding anniversary was around the corner and this would be her last married summer.

Now Edie May found the brown suitcase in the loft cupboard and the buckles snapped to attention when she opened it.

Married, she had once thought, meant joined together forever.

Jerry, twenty-two years old and inarticulately in love with her, staring at her midriff between her old white shirt and black shorts, and saying, 'They'll do it in North Dakota. Sneak your birth certificate into the suitcase.'

But first she had to graduate from high school and they had to save the deposit on an apartment, so they kept a brown plastic suitcase in his car and kept money in it and then a ring, and there was one more thing – his mother's white tablecloth that they made love on: once in a while they'd risk it on his living room floor.

Once, at one o'clock in the morning when they'd been kissing and kissing in her kitchen, suddenly the phone had rung and it was Jerry's dad: 'Your mother don't sleep good till you come home.'

It was right after that Jerry told her that he was worried about the draft and then about North Dakota.

The framed Polaroid that the justice of the peace's assistant had taken stayed on their dresser all those years, until the day he left for Cross Lake. Which was the end of something so vital to her life that she threw the frame down on the driveway and it stayed there until Rebecca picked up the glass, so nobody would get a puncture.

Now Edie had two separate thoughts.

First, her realization that she was never ready when men left her and she suffered too long afterwards. She was sick and tired of it.

Second, that tablecloth was a symbol of life with Jerry all spread out in front of her. He'd been everything — lover, brother, teacher. She'd put all her eggs in one basket and it had backfired when he came back from Nam and stopped really talking.

Maybe it was nobody's fault that there were things he didn't want her to know.

Well, she had secrets, too. Here was a good one: for three years now, since he'd left and they'd sold the house and she'd moved to Cambridge, she'd washed that tablecloth and dried it in the summer air and then slept with it on their anniversary night. It was sentimental, she always knew that, but it was only crazy if you believed that a man was going to come back to give your life meaning, or that your scapulas were going to bud into wings so you could fly around Angel's Pond in your faded denim dress.

She was a lot of things, but she wasn't crazy.

This was enough insight for Edie; you don't have to understand every aspect of a problem in order to solve it. Sometimes halfway measures are good enough.

Edie May went to Jerry's trailer one more time with the clear intention of discussing their divorce. She'd left a message on his phone the day before and took the tablecloth with her.

His truck wasn't in the driveway; his door was unlocked. She turned on the light over the stove and looked at dirty dishes in the sink. Waste paper basket full. Smell of old food. Not great, but not alarming.

And if she felt like Goldilocks when she sat in the armchair and tore the tablecloth in two, which was easy because she'd already cut it a few inches along the middle fold, that was all right until she realized she was staring at the sweatshirt on the back of a kitchen chair, small and pale green. It bothered her. She knew it was silly when you hadn't lived with your soon-to-be ex-husband for four years. It was just harder when you were on your own. Well, that was her own fault, wasn't it? Four years, she told herself. Plenty, plenty long.

She took a Leinenkugel beer out of the fridge and twisted the top open. Why wasn't Jerry answering his phone? She needed to talk to him before she lost her nerve. She stood in the middle of the trailer and sipped beer, which burned going down. The taste of summer, fading fast.

She wanted to believe that he'd left the door unlocked because he'd be back in a few minutes, but she knew he didn't use a key here; he had this idea about freedom.

She'd leave a note, keep trying his phone. She'd come back in a few days and start knocking on doors, if she had to. She could call Michael or Zac. But it wouldn't come to that.

She turned on the blue lights on her way out.

THE BAKERY, 2008

He didn't know why he stopped for her. She was walking along the shoulder of the highway, her back to him, on the wrong side of the road for pedestrians. She was wearing long shorts, and not exactly striding, but determined, and his first impulse was to give her plenty of room and accelerate past; but he found himself pulling over onto the shoulder fifty yards in front of her.

It was late morning, midweek. What made him stop? An empty road and some kind of hunger. He pushed it away, that irritation that sat in his gut on top of the cheap cornflakes he'd had for breakfast. In Lakeville he'd pick up groceries at the Town and Country and ask the guy at the meat counter for bones for Queenie.

He glanced over his shoulder. 'You soaking up the sun back there?', and the dog made eye contact, just one eye, like a wink because she'd been snoozing to the rhythm of the old station wagon. Steele wiped his warm face on his shirt-tail. How the car would smell to her – dirt, sweat, the fish he'd caught last night and wrapped in newspaper, a gift for Jerry who'd put a can half-filled with gas by his cabin door, and so Steele delivered fish first thing this morning.

He glanced in his mirror to see her peering into the rear window. 'Get ready, Queenie. We're having company.'

She walked up to the passenger seat and rested an arm on the open window. She was smiling, which embarrassed him. He was sorry he'd started this.

'Talking to your dog?'

'Queenie. She's back there on cushions, likes to ride like that.'

The woman leaned her head in and nodded. 'Great day. Wish I had a bike. Sam's got one, but it's too big for me.'

'He's rich enough to buy you one.'

When she laughed, he caught the smell of her soap or something she put on her skin and whatever it was, he liked it. Liked the way she'd taken off her sunglasses, as if it mattered to take a good look at his dog.

'My brother's not rich. He works hard for his money. He'll finish that house one day.' She paused. 'You're Steele, aren't you? I'm Cynthia. I recognize this old station wagon. It's usually parked next to your truck.'

'You're right.'

'I'm a walker. Walk all around The Point when I visit.'

'Staying long?'

'I stay longer now that Sam has a bigger place. I go back to teaching in September.'

'You're the one who lives in Europe.'

'England.'

'If you're heading for town, it's further than you think.'

'Six miles, isn't it? Told myself if I did it, then I'd treat myself to lunch. Where are you going?'

'Boring,' Steele answered. 'Hardware store – nails for my front steps, they're falling apart.' He tapped the steering wheel with his forefinger. 'Hop in, you made it halfway, it's hot out.'

They rode in silence for a few minutes. Oak trees and maples along the road, the sign for 'Maddie's Moorings', a glimpse of the lake.

When she chuckled to herself, he glanced over.

'I just noticed the sign on the tree back there advertising guns for sale. It's across the street from the funeral home. Sort of ironic, don't you think?'

'I guess. Where can I drop you?'

'Thought I'd try The Bakery, the place near the post office. What about you? Do you have time for lunch?'

'I've got all day but my money's in the freezer.'

'Is it?'

'I only bring out what I need.'

'Well, I can always lend you some.'

The Bakery was a wide rectangular building with a Western-style front porch, and two rocking chairs.

Steele turned off the motor. 'You go ahead. I'm letting Queenie out for a minute.'

She'd seen his tobacco pouch and papers on the dashboard; he needed a cigarette. Sam had called him a 'die-hard' smoker. Then added: 'Of course, if you'd lived through what he did, you'd need something to hang onto.' Cigarettes, booze, a little marijuana. Took the edge off. Kept the lid on. For a time.

Steele had been known to go on a bender. Sam told her how, just a month ago, he'd shouted his house down, tore the screen door off, then staggered down to the boat harbor to throw his empties at the water lilies. Sam had spent an hour waiting it out with him, not berating him, no judgment, finally saying: 'Maybe it's time to go inside now, Joe.' And Steele answering, 'Am I breaking the law? Well, am I? Since when are you the water lily police?' It made a funny story.

This going through her mind as she opened the door: the buzz of a café, the smell of a bakery. The glass case with baked goods next to the cash register so you could still be tempted when you paid your bill. She liked the big sofa in front of the fireplace, big mirror above the mantelpiece, magazines on a coffee table. She could stay all day.

Cynthia found a table in the corner, far enough away from an older couple reading the newspaper. Spacious, she thought, you'd need a lot of customers to pay the overheads. And then she remembered that she was here on vacation, and reached for the menu.

'So I begged Sam for one last swim before we drove to the airport. He stood on the dock and shouted that I'd miss my plane. Well, I flew home last year with lake hair and a wet costume in my suitcase.'

'Costume?'

'Swimsuit. That's what we call it.'

'Oh.'

It was a matter of talking about the lake because if she'd learned anything from her brother, it was that the lake was the Bachelors' focus. 'You couldn't live up here if you didn't love her,' that's what Sam said to her once, and Cynthia had answered, 'You talk as if the lake were your girlfriend.' So it was a matter of steering the conversation.

'How's your repair business going?'

'It's not a business. I help the guys out with their boats

41

and motors, and once in a while somebody knocks on my door who's willing to pay.'

She was reading the blackboard with the Specials. 'Look, the fish is supplied locally. That's sold me: fish sandwich and ice tea. What looks good to you?'

'Meatloaf on rye,' he replied. 'I eat fish all the time.' Steele closed his menu. 'Don't get me wrong. I like being out there, whether they're biting or not. Time slips away, like a fish off my hook.' He laughed softly, his eyes crinkling up. Where attraction starts.

He should laugh more, she thought, and watched him walk up to the counter to put in their order, then he circled to the coffee table and brought back a newspaper.

'So you're not vegetarian, Steele?'

'No, I eat anything, but I don't spend much money on steak. What about you? Are you one?'

'Only when it's to my advantage.'

Steele made eye contact, curious. 'What do you mean?'

'I cheat on the plane. They serve the special meals first and by the time they give us a drink, I'm starving, so I pre-book a vegetarian when I buy my ticket. One of these days the whole world will catch on and then I'll be responsible for a real mess.' She smiled to show him she wasn't serious. 'I do feel guilty about cheating, so I compensate by being really nice to the flight attendants. People are so rude. No please or thank you. It's need, instead of want. Since when do we *need* a Coke?'

'Wouldn't know. I don't like to fly.'

'It's over-rated. It's like taking a bus with spoiled brats.'

'But you like coming over here?'

She nodded. 'So I do it. Don't have a choice.'

'In the army, you didn't either. Go where they send you. Don't care if I never fly again.'

Cynthia looked at him carefully. 'No. I guess not.'

He opened the newspaper and they waited in silence.

They watched the baker bring over a tray with their drinks and food. This will help, she thought. She picked up her sandwich and dipped it in the tartar sauce.

'Why do you do that?'

'What?'

'Why not spread it on the bread?'

'So I'll eat less of it? So I'll be in control?' She was thinking how straight he sat in his chair, like he was on alert when she wanted him to relax. 'How's yours?'

'It looks good. I'm eating slow.'

'Good habit. I always slow down up here. In lots of ways.'

'That's what happens.'

'You know, last night when I walked back from the harbor, I'm sure I heard a loon. I haven't seen one for years but I know their call is sort of eerie; melancholy. Sam said it would have been a male.'

'Those northern divers stay around till the end of September. I catch their act out on the lake.'

'Really? I'd love to see one before I go back.'

And that hung in the air.

She turned her attention to her ice tea, to the baker woman bringing out a pie and placing it on the glass case to cool. A man who'd bought some baked goods carried his white bag out the door, and Cynthia saw through the window that he'd sat in one of the rocking chairs. For a moment she envied him because it was easier to be on your own.

'After lunch,' she said, 'I'm off to the post office for

stamps. Sam's writing checks and paying bills, and I still write postcards.'

'He likes you sending those.'

'How do you know that?'

'He puts them around his truck. His rig is like a museum. Once in a while he invites us in for some weird beer he's found. Whatever the road brings, he always says, I like to share.'

And Steele sounded – for a second – exactly like Sam. Sam, who didn't really let her in. Who was an honorary Bachelor because he wasn't a vet, but he was definitely a loner. Cynthia yawned. It was a closed club. 'Well, that's nice to hear.' She felt full, the blood rushing to her stomach. The walk back would do her good.

'When I was away, my mother wrote twice a month and made postcards.'

'She made them?'

'Magazine pictures on top of each other.'

'Collage. Did the shellac make them shiny?'

'Don't remember. Kept some. They're yellow now.'

She thought of his small cabin. How much of his past had he carried here? How much was burned, lost, scattered?

Steele said, 'You're easy to talk to.'

She waited.

'Hey,' he said. 'I know the best free coffee in town.'

'Just what I need,' she laughed. 'All right, where will you be?'

'Look for the car in the Town and Country lot. There's a little shade over on the side.'

In the time it took Steele to finish his lunch, he considered a hundred disparate things.

She'd taken it in her stride, that's how it looked to

him, climbing in with her long legs, picking up newspapers, envelopes, empty soda cans; and placing them on the floor before looking for the seatbelt. The buckle was caught underneath. He'd felt silly, that glimpse of his ramshackle vehicle through her eyes. And who needed a Coke? Well, he did. Every day.

Now Steele scraped his chair back on the wooden floor. He felt like a teenager; he wasn't used to eating in front of a woman. He wanted to share his food with Queenie; that's how they did it at home.

To hell with it. The meatloaf was good and the bread just baked, and he wrapped the last quarter in his napkin.

And now there'd be the bill and she'd walked outside like she'd forgotten all about it. What if he didn't have enough? What about if he asked her for her share so he could buy gas and maybe drive around the lake. Was that the right thing to do?

He looked into his glass of ice water. He fished out the lemon slice and bit into it, and suddenly he was thinking about his mother's lemonade where nothing was wasted. She'd made frugal look graceful. Steele took a cube into his mouth, his mother warning him not to chew it. He had nice teeth; he should take care of them.

The way she'd said it, simple and with love. It made him swallow hard. Ghosts on the road – something Jerry said once in a while about women who had cared for him, and Steele remembered the phrase because the image unnerved him.

If only he wasn't so out of practice.

And weren't the women on planes stewardesses? Flight attendant sounded like a soldier. But what did he know? Only that coming back on that military plane wasn't as simple as it looked. Changing onto a commercial jet in Los Angeles, the airport a jungle of its own, Vietnam fading temporarily into some kind of limbo hell, and then the stewardess quietly leaning over to verify his status. 'We're not used to seeing soldiers in civvies. There's a better seat for you up front.' And she'd given him a moment to gather himself, while she picked up his beer and he followed her to First Class, embarrassed that everyone was watching, that he hadn't done this right.

Maybe he couldn't do this: go back to where he came from.

He'd wanted to bury his face in the back of her neck.

'Your family meeting your plane? Well, there won't be any fuss. They've changed things, so you just disembark like everybody else.'

She'd never know that she'd been a bridge.

That he'd move to where there was a lake to lose himself in. He could fish all day.

Now Steele looked around and smiled: a good flashback, for a change. He had twenty dollars in his car for emergencies, and he wanted a cigarette.

He hoped she'd show up, but he wouldn't wait for her.

Cynthia leaned against the warm metal of the car door. He'd parked in the delivery driveway, in a piece of shade where no one parked because no one would want to walk that far. The windows were down; Queenie had changed positions on the cushions. Cynthia spotted a thermos bottle where the top, filled with water, had become the dog bowl.

Steele came walking toward them and as she looked into the sun she saw how lean he was in his jeans, cheekbones almost parallel with his hipbones.

He carried a cardboard box like a tray and looked

pleased with himself, shy.

'Hey Queenie, got your bones.'

'Asleep. I checked.'

He nodded and set the box on the hood and handed her a small, sturdy Dixie cup of black coffee. 'I didn't think you were the type who'd want fake cream.' Then gave her a paper napkin folded into a package; inside were two round donut holes. 'Day-olds,' he said. 'Good enough for my sweet tooth.'

'Mine too. Thanks.' She had a strange sensation of being rooted in the moment but pulled into the past. 'Why do I feel like I'm at the State Fair?'

He pointed at her cup. 'Are you thinking about the milk stand, all you could drink for a quarter? Everybody bought their bag of Tom Thumbs for dunking. We farm kids could drink a lot. Cups were small but we kept going back.'

'Where did you grow up?'

'Aitkin, north of here. Ya, taking our chickens to the big cities was a vacation. Only reason I stuck with 4-H was the Fair – and to meet girls.'

She laughed, set down her cup. 'It's still hot.'

'Let's take a drive and stir the air around.'

'I meant the coffee, but I'd like to. And I owe you some money.' She reached for her backpack.

They drove west around the lake.

But first, he drove down a side street near the high school, unremarkable until he explained that this was the location of the former creamery which had been near the train station.

How did he know that?

They were going to open a small museum; someone had donated a homesteader's house, 1915. It was in the paper where they'd printed a photo of the old creamery on White Pine Avenue. Except that street name didn't exist now. But Steele had figured out the original site. They could change the names all they wanted, he told her – Fourth Street, Fifth Street – but they couldn't move the pines.

What did Sam say about Steele? 'Great eyesight. Not much insight.' With his unreadable gray eyes, she was deciding, Steele didn't miss much.

In front of the high school they sat quietly. He rolled a cigarette. Queenie paced in the back, leaned her head to nuzzle Steele's shoulder. 'She's ready to get out. I know where we can go.' He lit his cigarette and leaned back to smoke.

She looked at him, remembered that they sent him into the tunnels first, to make sure it was safe, and when Cynthia had pushed Sam for details, Sam glared at her. 'If I knew what he found, do you think I'd tell you? He came back alive; he wants the rest buried.' But she'd read enough to know you couldn't come out of Vietnam unscathed. Buried, maybe, but not gone.

He took her to Freddy's, the resort that was modernizing itself with lots of amenities, hoping for the younger crowd. 'Thrown a lot of money at it. Hauled sand down from Duluth to widen the beach. Built two docks. Finally opened for the Fourth of July.'

'Did you go?'

'No. Hung out at the Jacksona, more my style.'

'I know where that is, Sam took me once. But mainly, he likes to stay home.'

'Can't blame him, all the driving he does.'

'You're right. He mows the lawn for fun. What about

you?'

'Fun? I row my rowboat.'

'Two boats. Two vehicles.'

'One frying pan. One life.'

'You don't believe in reincarnation?'

He laughed and said, 'Go ahead and look around. I'm taking the dog for a walk.'

Cynthia stood at the end of the dock and stared at the lake. She'd love to go swimming. If she'd known, she would have worn her matching black underwear — who could tell? She'd done that in Miami, and in Barcelona had slipped off her bra as well.

Now she watched him on the beach with Queenie. They looked happy. She wished he'd take off his shoes, and then thought: Leave them be.

She took off her own shoes and dangled her feet in the water. She lay on the dock and removed her sunglasses, then covered her face with the hat she pulled out of her backpack. She must have slept because when she woke up, she was disoriented, her white hat over her eyes made winter sky and her feet were warming by a fireplace. It only lasted a second. She was awake in an endless summer afternoon.

She looked around and found them stretched out under a tree near the parking lot.

It had been a long time since he'd watched anybody sleep, never mind a woman. When she walked over, Steele said, 'Nice hat.'

'It protects my hair from the sun.'

He wanted to touch her hair. But it would be like lighting a candle in church when you didn't believe.

'Did you take a siesta?' she asked.

'Closed my eyes. Can't sleep during the day.'

The tree was an old oak, big enough for both of them to sit and lean against. She stood and said, 'For a second, out there on the dock, I forgot it was summer.'

'How could you?'

'When I woke up, I saw white. I usually see colors.'

'What about now?'

She closed her eyes. 'Lime green. Chartreuse *is* summer.'

'I'm better with smell. I smell things before I see them.'

'Like what, Joe?'

'Dead fish and rain.'

'What else?'

'I can smell trouble.' Then he smiled. 'But most of the time I smell the next season before I see any signs of it.'

'I know what you mean. I always breathe in that hint of fall here, just when I'm getting ready to go back to school. Then I decorate my classroom with loads of paper leaves.' She paused. 'You probably didn't like school. You're an outdoors guy.'

While they were talking, a large flat launch boat had sidled up to the second dock. The boat, with its wooden canopy, took twenty people fishing and was a tradition, left over from the days when fewer people owned boats. New passengers climbed on board and Steele watched the launch pull away like a missed opportunity.

'We could go in and have a beer,' he said.

She squinted at him. 'It's too early.'

Spoken like an authority figure, he thought, and watched her sit down and lean against the tree. Steele sighed. 'School was my job so my mother could go to hers. It was just me and her and I couldn't let her down.'

'Who was your favorite teacher?'

'Fifth grade. Miss Ellison moved me up to the green reading group. Never said that it was better than blue or yellow. Only that all colors come from nature, and nature is perfect.'

'Those were her words?'

'Something like that. She had them on a banner over the blackboard. The thing is, I got better at reading and so it was easier. I got good enough so the other kids stopped picking on me.' He smiled, liking the memory. 'If she heard the bullies call me Dumb Joey, she'd call them by the wrong name. They hated that. Everybody loved Miss Ellison.'

He glanced at her to make sure she was listening.

'I waited for her to stop being nice to me – for it to fall apart.' He stared at the lake. 'Her cat was hit by a car. Hit and run. She cried. The day before Christmas vacation, right before the concert, and she couldn't hold it in. She said the milkman delivered it to her, sad and snow-flecked. Ya, those were her words.'

'What happened?'

'I must have been moping around at home because my mother got the story out of me. Then she walked over to her desk and wrote out a card. She had to make a few phone calls to find out the address.'

Cynthia wanted to ask what his teacher's first name was.

But Steele didn't give her a chance, he talked on, piecing something together. 'We all went back to school in January, and it got colder. At home our old furnace was struggling. One morning Miss Ellison asked why my lips were blue and later on during supper, one of the janitors knocked on our door.'

He had gone quiet for a moment. 'She took me to the State Spelling Bee that spring. We did okay.' Then he looked at Cynthia. 'Hey, you're bored. Don't know how I got into that.'

'I'm not bored,' she said.

Steele had parked in the shade and now that the afternoon was three degrees closer to evening, the inside of the car was bearable. He had perspiration patches on his shirt and her hair felt lank. She stared out the window as he drove. She accepted the bottle of water he bought her at the gas station and knew better than to offer money.

She saw a sign: 'Local Wild Rice For Sale'. She always took some home and he'd know the best places to buy it. He might even know where it grew, but the image of a rice field stopped her. 'Slow down up here,' that's what he'd said to her. But there was slow and there was stricken. There were men you'd like to try talking to for the rest of your life, and sometimes these were men you shouldn't talk to at all.

'I like this side of the lake,' she said. 'I like exploring.'

When he pulled into Angel's Pond, she watched his attention turn to the harbor. He took his hands off the wheel for a second and pushed up invisible sleeves, preparing to work.

'My rowboat should be ready next week. Queenie's excited.'

Did she care? Yes, despite the fact that she lived in another country most of the year; that she might hate the frozen blue winters up here; that he would never have any money and didn't belong anywhere except out on the lake by himself. Did he ever cry out there?

'Thanks, Joe.' Cynthia smiled.

'It was okay.'

Sam was sitting outside his house on a lawn chair, with his radio. He waved as Steele turned his car around. As she walked toward her brother, he said to her, 'Been gone awhile.'

'Lost track of time. We were talking.'

But he followed her into the house and said, 'Steele lives on his nerves, Cynthia, so don't think you can go digging out his feelings. They're buried in blood and guts.'

'Don't be so dramatic, Sam.'

'He's not good with women. Stop messing with him. I mean it.'

Women, Steele believed, were mostly like Miss Ellison, not sure what to do with their love. They could melt away; he was afraid of that. Miss Ellison had looked melted and lost for months.

And he'd seen it in Nam, little girl whores who gave as much as they could, hoping for a better life in some unpronounceable state. Veesconsin. Meechgun.

He left Minnesota out of it, but why lie about where he was from? Love and war had that in common: you didn't react rationally. He remembered during training and even when he'd first been flown over, how they all talked about the war, argued, the morality of it on the tips of their tongues. But the longer he stayed, the less was said. Instead, they talked impersonally about the gooks and the assholes in Washington and, in spite of themselves, they voiced what they missed: the simple wordless joy of waking up in your own bed. But that carried its own pain and at those times it wasn't so bad in the tunnels where his senses were on alert, but he could stay silent. Yes, he might die, but then his reputation would soar home on an angel flight, and rifles would be fired into the air and his buddies would say grandiose things to his mother and that wouldn't have been so bad for her, would it?

Steele shook his head. He was destined to keep living, but he didn't want much to do with women. Love: if you fell in, you climbed out.

PHILLUMENY, 2007

At the wedding reception Renee stood behind the bar, selling hard liquor, and watched the guests pile their plates from the buffet table and help themselves to kegs of beer. By eight o'clock she'd glimpsed the start of a fight. And whether the radiant couple were meant for each other, who could say? She wanted to be happy for them and so she was. Tonight was All Hallow's Eve at the run-down Jacksona on Cross Lake; what more could they want?

Renee sipped her mint tea. The middle-aged man came and stood in front of her and ordered a brandy and Coke. He said, 'This is the strangest wedding party I've ever been to. But I sort of like this place. What's it like working here?'

'I don't know yet,' she smiled. 'I'm doing the owner a favor tonight. But I can tell you that the sinks plug up fast and we could use a better ice machine.'

The man smiled back. 'It needs some attention. A real fire hazard, people smoking inside.'

'Well, that's Sandy Jackson for you.'

'Is he looking to sell? I've got someone who wants to invest on this lake.' He picked up a book of matches from the box on the bar, glanced at its black cover with orange writing:

> 'Diane and Steve
> October 31st 2007
> Happily Ever After
> Spooky!'

She could feel him looking at her, wondering where she fit in. She almost wished she hadn't worn her shaped black jeans and boots or washed her hair. She'd always liked the nights that men looked straight through her, but she knew enough to make a good impression.

'You're not from here,' he said to her.

'Neither are you.' His dark green jacket, new. His fingernails, clean. A contrast to the two men in old jeans at the corner table sprawled on folding chairs; one with his chair facing backward, like a cowboy playing poker.

A latecomer had walked in then, greeted his friends in the corner before he made his way to her, put his hand in his pocket and dumped bills and change on the bar. 'Let me know when I've drunk this up,' he'd said. 'If you'd be so kind to an old man.'

How he managed this without looking at her. Not until he was on his third whiskey did he ask her name and even then his eyes were shielded. Or maybe it was the way he turned, looked back to the table, and the cowboy called out something coded that sounded like: 'Throw her back, Jerry, she's too tall for you.'

Renee stayed calm. She stayed busy though most of the guests were taking advantage of free beer. The man in the green jacket wanted to converse a little more. And if the locals stopped talking when she walked between the tables collecting glasses, well, she was the new girl and on her best behavior.

Not that her boss was watching. She couldn't find him when she needed help with the ice machine. Then she saw him across the room talking to Mr Green Jacket. Later he stood with his arm around the bride, she in her jeans and a red floor-length coat. Then he disappeared with her. Renee was sure of it. She drank her tea and remembered how bizarre and depressing it could be when you were the only sober person in the room.

Jerry was outside on the bench facing the lake, sobering up so he could drive. That's what she thought as she took in a long breath; she hadn't been outside for hours. He was shining his flashlight around. The moon was half full; and there was the sound of Sandy's boat bumping against the dock.

His voice shot through the dark. 'Over here.' He was careful not to shine too close to her. 'Sit down. Take a load off.'

'No thanks. I'm going home.' She held a plate, covered with aluminum foil. 'I'm hungry.'

'Ya, let's go back to your place.'

'You've had a lot to drink.'

'You shouldn't pour them so strong.'

'I just pour them. Nothing special tonight.' Wasn't going to mention that Sandy had hinted to go easy on the shots.

She took a look at him: on the edge of haggard. Saw his stomach hanging over his belt and old moccasins with duct tape around the front of one.

He was watching her, but listlessly. 'Whatever Jackson's paying you, he'll get his money's worth. Tight like his dad was. Both a little crazy. It was a good party, though.' As if producing evidence, he shone the light on the pumpkin in the birdbath.

The couple had arrived in Sandy's boat, with Sandy driving fast, and even Renee had walked outside to see. All three dressed in jeans and long coats. The groom carried the pumpkin; the bride threw flowers and leaves to her friends.

'He takes his boat out later than anyone else. It's dangerous, but the maverick does it anyway.'

'So this was a family business?'

'Ya, but it's been open and closed a dozen times since Sven died. Sandy doesn't have the head for business. He's better with machines than people. Likes to keep his old truck going to drive around, picking up rent checks.'

'Rent checks?'

'Family property. Cabins. Two near Loon Mission.'

'Where do you live?'

'East side near Angel's Pond. That's the official name, but we call it Bachelors Road.'

'Which Bachelor tried to start the fight?'

She watched his face close. 'Hey, those are my neighbors. Socializing. That's what weddings are for, right?'

She'd been careless because she was tired. A woman in men's territory. 'I'm a fish out of water here.'

'Aw, you'll learn.'

And they both laughed.

Two days later she found herself driving over to the east side to find Angel's Pond. Had he hooked her when he told her all the trees were rusting? She could come out and see.

His directions helped. She brought soup and crackers and the pumpkin.

When she arrived, he handed her a map of the lake left over from the summer season. She looked around his trailer: male and minimal. When she looked at him, she saw how he still might be handsome if he didn't look so resigned.

When he pointed to the pumpkin, she said, 'Let's carve it.'

But his knives weren't sharp enough. And what would they do with it, anyway?

'It's just for fun, Jerry. Don't you remember carving jack-o'-lanterns?'

But he looked lost, like he'd never get back to his childhood. And she felt that familiar, tiresome feeling in her stomach. She could use some men friends up here but he would not be a contender.

They did take a walk, though, past the other beat-up trailers and one lake cabin with its own dock, then around to The Point so she could get the scope of it, how the wind came from either direction so one side was rough water when the other was calm. He pointed out their boat harbor named Angel's Pond and, tucked into the trees, three retirement homes. One belonged to a truck driver who was away half the year.

They were circling back to his place again.

He said, 'Cross Lake is a love-it-or-hate-it lake.'

She was careful what she said. 'So which Bachelors love it here?'

'Dwayne. The loud mouth.'

She remembered.

'Steele is down by Red Eye Resort on a cheap lot. The further you are from the lake, the less tax you pay. We old veterans need that.'

So that was it, what was buried deep.

'What about Sandy? Is he a vet?'

'No. Got out of that one.'

She glanced at Jerry: no further information.

'You should drive around the entire lake, Renee; that's what the map is for. Acclimatize.' He lowered his voice as if his advice was important. And he made it sound like she'd be staying.

Well, was she? She liked it here, low-key and small-town, no other acupuncturists for miles. Time to get her courage up and take the business plan forward.

Sandy laughed out loud when she told him she was staying in the apartment block in Lakeville. He said, 'They rent those rooms out by the hour, don't they? And who wants to live across from the funeral parlor?'

He was making fun. Then: 'Listen, I have places that need living in. One's only ten minutes from the Jacksona. Insulated, fumigated, and the furnace goes like crazy. Maybe we can come to an agreement.'

She agreed to try it for two nights. Saw that the housette, as he'd called it, was warm and private. She liked the iron radiators, and her front gate where the yard rolled downhill, then across the road to lakeshore neighbors. At the back she had access to a slip road and plenty of parking.

On the minus side: the place needed cleaning, and Sandy would need to charge less than for an apartment because her savings needed to last the winter.

Renee opened the front door, looked down to the lake. She stood and ate her bowl of oatmeal. The breeze through the screen door cooled her legs. He'd been so relieved when she hadn't balked at the state of the kitchen that he'd given her two weeks' free rent. Then: 'Stay the winter and work. We'll go slow through December and open for ice fishing.'

She phoned Andrew in Des Moines who listened as always.

'So your boss is also your landlord. If both of you can handle that, you've got a plan, Renee. I know you've bought insurance, but make sure his premises are covered and that he's okay with you working there.'

She missed Andrew, the friend she'd made on the course, and his logical thinking. He was practical, patient and intuitive.

Now on the phone he reminded her about the continuing education course for graduates in January. 'Read the information. Plan on staying with me again.'

'I'd love to, thanks. How's your love life, Andy? You working on it?'

The night they'd sat on his living room carpet and drank champagne and spoken about the future. He planned to practice in a clinic. Outside of work, he planned to meet men. 'I'm more attracted to men,' he'd said. 'I'm tired of fighting it.'

She wanted to drive straight north of Des Moines and live somewhere different; she was tired of Iowa. In her mind, she needed to leave behind her dried-up, small-town reputation. Tough Renee in the bathroom of Hefner's Department Store, taking out of the bag the same skirt she had on, but smaller, so tight she'd unpicked the seam where the skirt was split at the bottom, so she could still walk down the street and talk to the boys.

She called her high school senior year the 'Dance of the Twin Skirts'.

Now she knew that you could approach your life with integrity. It had taken her years to feel comfortable with herself. By herself. And so fifteen pounds would come and go, and the fact remained that she was thinner when there was a man in the picture. She still owned skirts and jeans in two different sizes, but she'd stopped worrying about it when her acupuncture course started.

Now Andrew was saying, 'Keep in touch and find some clients.' He meant: *Don't lose your nerve*.

She followed through and invited Sandy to come over.

'We have something to talk about,' she said. 'I'm also an acupuncturist. You need to know that.'

'Whoa. Who would have guessed?'

'I qualified in July. I'd like to see clients here.'

He looked her up and down. 'Is it dangerous?'

'No, but I'd be burning candles and Moxa sticks because some people prefer cupping to needles.'

He took his time before he said, 'There's no point selling it unless you hang around to reap the benefits. So you'll be staying through next summer. Let's sit and write down some numbers.'

'As far as insurance goes, I have personal indemnity.'

'Okay.'

'What about you, Sandy?'

'Heaps of insurance. A whole filing drawer.'

'So don't look so nervous. I'll have plenty of time to work for you.'

Their agreement: bartending Thursdays through Sundays. And if she wanted to earn more, the bar and restaurant needed cleaning.

She told him she'd keep track of her hours.

Renee the Resolute, he called her, and she wasn't sure she liked that.

The end of the afternoon. The gate clinked shut.

Jerry had been sent to put the storm door on. Renee was not unhappy to see him standing there. He stamped his boots, shaking off dirt, as if he knew she was transforming the place.

He looked around. 'The woman's touch.'

She smiled. She looked awful, had crawled out of bed and into old clothes. 'You're my first visitor. Would you like to sit down?'

'I'll do the door while it's light.'

She was conscious of them working alongside each other as she unpacked a box of books. When he took the screen door out to the shed, she slipped into the bathroom to slick on lipgloss.

Then she asked him to help move the couch into the corner; she turned on the lamp.

'Looks good, Renee.'

'I've worked all week. But sometimes when you're too close, you can't see your progress.'

She brought from the kitchen two glasses, a can of Coke, an almost-empty bottle of rum. She said, 'I think these glasses are crystal.'

He traced the pirate on the rum label with his finger. 'How long's this been around?'

'One of many things I've found. It still tastes good.'

He leaned toward the coffee table and simply looked at his glass.

'Jerry?'

'I don't drink the first week of the month.'

'Okay. Any special reason?'

'It's a survival thing, too easy to go downhill.'

'Like me drinking mint tea in the bar.'

He smirked at her. 'Can't see you losing control.'

She looked into the room that was meant to be a

dining room, bare except for a bookcase and her treatment table.

'What do you think? Enough privacy for massage?'

'Massage? Is that what you're up to?'

'Trained years ago, but I recently finished an acupuncture course.'

'That weird thing with needles?'

'It's more common than you'd think.'

'So you don't like doctors?'

'Western medicine is not good for everything.'

'Like what?'

'Migraines, back pain, insomnia.'

'Two out of three's not bad. But you have to get them in the door, and winter's hibernation time. Not many people around.'

'Sandy told me. That's why I'm tending bar. I can start small.'

'Did he volunteer to take off his clothes and be your guinea pig?'

'He's my boss. I wouldn't encourage him. Anyway, I could use your opinion about this.' When she returned from the kitchen, she had her notebook and pen. 'If you had something you wanted help with, and you saw this card, what would you think?'

'Renee's Retreat
Massage & Acupuncture
near Cross Lake
470 White Rock Road
(parking in the back)
651 204 6695.'

'Retreat? Sounds like a commune or a brothel.'

'Good point. Anything else?'

'Don't give out your address until they make an appointment. But make the phone number bigger. Reel them in.'

She laughed and, if she'd broken the ice with him, it was because he allowed it. He was slow, cool, whereas Sandy was greasy and quick and might be hard to keep at arm's length. She had more to learn about this place and the men connected to it.

Jerry took the rum bottle home; said he liked pirates. She told herself that she was too old to read meaning into inanimate objects.

Jerry told his cousin Zac, on the phone, that Renee was statuesque. He thought she'd be good in bed, kept that to himself, and said, 'She does massage and stuff.'

'Glad to hear it. Can she help you rise from the dead?'

Jerry heard his cousin chuckle at his own innuendo.

Jerry's arm was bothering him; it ached at night in the cold. Maybe she could help. He didn't share this, though he was as close to Zac as to anybody. They were eleven and twelve the summer Zac's parents included Jerry on their family vacation to Cross Lake where the boys built a fort named Pirate's Hill. They took their shirts off and welcomed sunburn, stuck grass in their cheeks like tobacco. Zac, who took Jerry hunting when he came back from Vietnam and re-introduced him to Cross Lake, that expanse of water so different from the jungle. Where neither of them had tried very hard to shoot a deer.

Now, years later, they picked up from wherever they'd left off.

'So, Jer, you'll be spending more time at the Jacksona. How is the old joint? I'll come up for ice fishing.'

When she collected her business cards from the print shop in town which was connected to the newspaper, she'd kept the conversation going with the young man at the counter because you never knew — he might need acupuncture or his mother might.

He said, 'Why don't you also take out an ad in our paper? I can offer a discount.'

'I'll try the cards first.'

'Sure. The bakery, the hardware store, the laundromat all have bulletin boards.'

Things were moving slowly, but moving.

This is what she found on the shelves under the bar, the morning she tackled them with Brillo pads. A framed photo of Sandy's father, in cold weather gear, holding up a walleye pike, both of them frozen. Sven, the businessman, with his Iowa clientele, fishermen who returned with their families in the summer. She could read 'JACKSONA' on the boathouse in clear white letters, the way it would have been seen from the lake, a landmark.

She found a container with a myriad of matchbooks: used, new, local, out-of-town. She laid them on the bar and wiped them off. Laughed at the one with the phone number scrawled on the inside cover: 'You could do worse – 783 2128'.

Sandy picked up two matchbooks and shook them like dice. 'Throw this old stuff away.'

'Sandy,' she said, 'a little nostalgia wouldn't hurt.'

'So now you're an interior designer?'

'Why not use what you have?'

'Stop telling me what to do.' His unshaven face, vulnerable. He'd raised his voice. 'I don't have diplomas on the wall like you. But I know a lot. Listen to this. Phillumeny: the fantastic collection of matchbox covers.'

Renee stayed quiet.

'I did crosswords on the toilet in the morning before school. My mother begged those newspapers from the neighbors. Sometimes my old man timed me.'

'Why?'

'He wanted me to be smart and know how to push myself.'

'Sounds lonely. Any brothers or sisters?'

Sandy shook his head. 'A dog. And in the summers I had the farmers' kids to play with. They stayed in our cabins, used the dock. They liked my mother's decent food in the restaurant.'

'And you were the waiter?'

'The bus boy, the boat boy, the fish cleaner boy-oh-boy.'

'You worked hard.'

'I left and came back. More than once.' He smiled a tired smile. 'Then one day they were old and needed my help.'

When Sandy licked his lip, Renee saw him three-dimensional, part of a family and rooted to this lake.

'Now I've got cabins for rent. I don't make any money when they're empty.'

'What about advertising on matchbooks?'

'No, that's old-fashioned.'

'What about a business card, Sandy? I've just had one printed.' She handed one to him.

He ran his thumb down the line of Chinese characters. 'Word of mouth always worked before.'

She looked him in the eyes. 'That was before. Thought I'd leave some on the bar, if that's okay.'

'Good luck.'

November settled in, making the men hunched over and lazy. They played cards with indifference, nursed their beers for dear life. Sandy started smoking menthol cigarettes, said it was a winter thing because he missed being outside. He helped himself to the matchbook collection in the bowl on the bar. She'd figured him out though because one day she saw his stash in a little plastic bag on his desk: he needed help mellowing out, but drinking didn't work when you were the proprietor. And that old couch in Sandy's office: it was there for a reason.

One day she heard him slam his filing cabinet shut. When she went in to look, he'd dumped two drawerfuls of paper on the floor. She burst out laughing. 'Before you file them, take them out of the envelopes. Where's your shredder? I'll make confetti for the next wedding.'

Thanksgiving with light snow came and went, along with dirty paper plates and high spirits and jokes about the place looking brighter. 'It's because she's been cleaning all the lights,' Sandy grinned.

One day he walked over to her with his calendar and asked when she was leaving for her Christmas vacation.

'It's not really a vacation,' she said. 'I'm visiting my brother, then doing a course at the university in early January.'

'Why don't you come to Florida with me instead?'

And she ignored that.

When Renee returned in January, the weather had shifted and snow stuck to the trees. Wind, ruthless and angry, blew across the highway as she drove in.

Christmas seemed long ago. In Muscatine, she'd visited her brother's family and walked down to the river she'd grown up with, but now – with a huge lake to compare it to – the river had narrowed. She'd driven around town, parked across from Oscar's, the supper club where she'd worked when she started learning massage. It was where she'd decided that the skills needed for bartending, for masseuse work, as well as for sleeping around were pretty much the same: pretending you liked them and giving them what they wanted. She'd kept her apron; it was a symbol the way the twin skirts were a memory.

Her real celebration was in Des Moines with Andrew. She was happy to be sleeping on his sofa bed again. He brought her tea, cooked delicious food, and gave her a gift of two expensive candles. 'To keep you calm,' he said, 'with your new clients.'

She lit the cinnamon and fig immediately, then handed him a bag of wild rice grown near Cross Lake.

On New Year's Eve she found herself in an apartment with Andrew's new friends, two men who'd found each other later in life. Eight stories above the city, she walked around touching Christmas ornaments. At the table, she raised her glass to friendship and the bright lights of Des Moines below. 'And good luck on your course,' the hosts added. Renee was as ready to see Mercy College again as she could be.

Throughout the week, she felt like an acupuncturist. She sat in the front and asked questions, chose people to work with she didn't know at all. She and Andrew read through their notes each evening. Drank a glass of red wine to relax. Agreed that happiness was what you felt last thing at night when you were involved in something meaningful, when you weren't fixated on results.

'The invisible line to happiness,' Renee said quietly one night, looking up from her laptop.

As she packed to leave he said, 'You've worn that sweater all week, you might as well keep it.'

It covered her Christmas pounds well.

At the gas station she bought a cup of coffee and a cup of hot chocolate and sipped until she was satisfied. Then she'd locked her doubts in her trunk and drove out.

Someone had shoveled off a parking space, shoveled a path to the door. The kitchen light was on. A piece of transparent film had been taped to the kitchen window, covering the sill where a draft wiggled in.

Sandy – who'd left a message on New Year's Eve: 'Come back, all is forgiven.' Barely audible with noise and music in the background. 'The lake's freezing over. It's talking to us, Renee. It sort of cackles. Hey, we're fixing up the fish house. You can come to our opening,' Sandy slurred, and then somebody had maybe grabbed the phone because it wasn't okay – a woman turning up to the Bachelors' ritual.

That night she moved back into her housette. She'd brought back Iowa calendars, hung one up, saved two for the Jacksona. She kept the lights low. How simple it was to turn a room into a refuge. She thought of all the rented places she'd lived in. They'd made it easier to move on.

Dwayne and Steele were busy running their Drift Dippers business. They told Renee how last year they'd fitted a snow blade onto Dwayne's truck, scooped out a few driveways. This year they'd invested in having 'DRIFT DIPPERS' painted on the side of the door, with a phone number, for when you found yourself out in a storm and drifted into the ditch.

Bachelors Road of course was the clearest road around and they couldn't wait to plow half a mile out in front of the Jacksona so fishermen could drive out onto the lake.

The day they pushed Sandy's lilac fish house onto its runners and towed it out was the day the men's eyes were as bright as children's.

The event was planned for one o'clock. Jerry and Sandy were working in the kitchen under the sink, killing time, when Renee walked in. Did they stop talking when they heard her?

'Am I interrupting? Don't stop. I might learn something. By the way,' she laughed, 'it's the sink in the bar I need unplugged.'

'We're doing both,' Jerry greeted her. 'I was just saying this place is falling apart. So don't get too attached.'

Sandy had crawled out to look at her. 'Cold weather: bad for plumbing, good for fishing.'

'Can you look at the men's toilet?' Renee asked. 'It keeps running.'

'How do you know that?'

'Who do you think cleans it?'

At noon they loaded the trucks with fishing gear, an auger to drill out ice holes, a propane heater, liquor to warm them up, folding chairs, camp bed, cooler.

The first ritual: Dwayne, Steele, Jerry and Sandy stood outside their trucks and chugged two beers apiece, then passed the schnapps around, one warming hit each.

'Whoo—ee,' they sang out. 'Let's really go.'

By the time they'd found the perfect location for the fish house, they'd need to take a leak. And the tradition was to piss their initials on the snow. The man with the largest letters won.

With a straight face Sandy told her this.

Renee asked, 'What exactly do you win?'

'You just win, sweetheart. Don't you have some floors to mop?'

Dismissed, just like that. She'd watched the convoy drive onto the ice and turn into small bugs crawling along the horizon. She itched with irritation. Why the hell was he so rude? Who did he think he was?

Renee went back inside and looked at the mess in the kitchen: tools scattered on the floor, a knife stuck into the jar of peanut butter. It could stay that way. She was going into town to check out The Bakery café and see if any of her cards had been removed. She'd devised a way of stringing a few together; it was easy to tear one off. She planned to introduce herself to the other owner if she was on the premises, or at least talk to some customers, if she wasn't.

And Renee would have recovered her equilibrium if her furnace hadn't gone silent and hostile the next afternoon. She'd switched it off and on again the way that Sandy had shown her and then banged it hard with her hand because she'd have to ask him for help and she didn't want to. She hadn't wanted to go ice fishing, but it would have been nice to have been asked. For a moment she was back in high school where she'd been excluded from the girls' cliques, so turned to the boys.

Renee looked down at her hands. That old skin she was still shedding. She considered the cookies in the cupboard, the scale in the bathroom. Instead of comfort eating, she straightened her back and reached for her phone. She paid rent, so she'd ring her landlord.

When Renee heard a truck outside, she opened the door for Jerry. She'd wound her red scarf around her shoulders like a shawl and left the oven door open to heat the kitchen. She followed him over to the furnace where he sniffed, checking for gas. Then he knelt down to look at the controls.

'So you phoned Sandy and got no answer. Is that it?'

'I didn't know who else to call.'

'He's in bed, hungover. So was I. My tools are in the truck, but I'd hate to get this wrong.'

'Please try.'

'Any spare fuses around?' When he stood up, he winced as he put his hand against the wall to steady himself. 'I was drilling ten-inch holes when I should have been under the electric blanket.'

Renee smiled. She'd heard the Bachelors teasing him about his hibernation strategy. Pictured him sitting up watching TV.

'It's warm, but lonely. So I turn my blue lights on for company.'

Blue lights. It wasn't much to go on, but his soft side stirred her. *The trees are rusting.* Wasn't that what he'd said last fall, enticing her down to Bachelors Road where he was hiding out, hurt in ways she couldn't imagine. The war. The marriage he didn't talk about. But twice she'd seen him cradle his arm as if it were in a sling. She couldn't save him, she wasn't responsible for him, but she could help.

'Your arm hurts. Let me try something.'

'Not getting on that massage table.'

'All right, the couch.'

First, he found a fuse and cleaned the filter, re-set the timer, listened to the furnace. She closed the living room drapes. He lay on the couch in his tough wool socks and she knelt on a pillow alongside. Keep him talking, she thought.

The warden was checking permits. They'd only bought two and were pushing their luck with six lines. And Sandy had won the pissing contest. 'He cheated,' Jerry added. 'Found a water bottle when I shoveled snow.'

She shook her head as she massaged his arm.

'He cheats at everything.'

'Jerry, we need to unblock the energy in your arm. Help the qi flow.'

'No needles.'

'Not yet.' She wanted to work on the point below his elbow, Arm Three Miles. 'Anyway, the needles are so thin, you'll only feel a tingling.'

He had half-closed his eyes; it gave her a chance to study him. Old acne scars, slightly puckered skin. Was life hard for him even then? She knew him so little. Trusted him a fraction more.

'Slightly more pressure now.'

'That hurts.'

Afterwards, she let him drift, not sure if he was too guarded to sleep. She wanted to trace the line that ran from his nose to his mouth and deepened when he smiled. She lay his jacket over him and lit her candle. She needed to think about the ethics of where this was going. Maybe, as long as she was just doing massage, it was okay. When she heard a vehicle outside, she thought: No. Not now.

An insistent knock on the back door which was dead-bolted from inside; she hoped he didn't bring his key.

Then a rap on the kitchen window, then a triple bang on the front door. The wind followed him around the corners of the house.

Sandy's voice: 'You in there? Answer the door? Three hots and a cot. Understand? I do.'

There was belligerence that she'd not heard before.

'He's on one,' Jerry said softly. 'No point talking to him. Take it from me.'

Renee's stomach was a knot. They waited.

Sandy shouted out one more time: 'Three hots and a cot.' Then he kicked the door hard. His truck pulled away much too fast.

They sat in silence for a few moments. When Jerry pulled his jacket on, Renee walked into the bathroom to rinse her face.

He called, 'I'm going to make sure his truck isn't in the ditch.'

'What did he mean, Jerry?'

'Nothing. It was just talk.'

Renee leaned against the doorway. 'Explain. Three hots and a cot.'

'Aw, it's a man's world up here. The winter gets long.'

'Keep going.'

'You dream about staying with someone so you have three square meals—'

She did not look away.

'Come on, a warm bed is nice in the winter.'

'So that's what you talked about out there? And my name came up.'

'No, I wouldn't let it.'

'I'd love to believe you, but why should I?' She sighed. 'Go find him. That's what you do for each other up here.'

What she saw on the bar when she walked into the Jacksona the next day: the portable radio next to a bottle of malt liquor, next to a pack of cigarettes. The two-day-old mess in the kitchen, plus plates newly laced with dried egg. She stepped around it, into the restaurant.

Sandy stood, hands shoved in pockets, staring out at the lake. His dirty hair hung over one eye.

'I owe you,' he said. 'You sent Jerry to find me.'

'No, he was determined to go.'

'Was he?' And for a second he let her see. He'd been a fool and knew it.

When he pushed his hair back, she saw his raw hands. 'Did you lose your gloves, Sandy?' Renee was furious and felt sorry for him at the same time. 'It's pathetic the way you take such shit care of everything.'

'While you fly around like the Good Fairy, making improvements.' Sandy put his palm against the window frame. 'Clean windows. What for? We don't use this room.'

'To let the light in.'

'Don't get mystical on me.'

'I'm not! This place could be better. Why waste it?'

He didn't answer, but she knew. It was the Jacksona, occupation linked to identity.

She said, 'Sven was hard on you, but you told me he loved it here. And so do you.'

'Ya? We built those frames one blister-hot summer. Five layers of varnish in two days to make them indestructible.'

'And the frames have lasted, the windows still fit. What are you so angry about? Make a decision, Sandy. If you're staying, do something. And if you're going, then let somebody else have it.'

'I'm sorry I got you into this.'

'Into what?'

'Doesn't matter.'

'Well, I'm not leaving.'

'I don't want you to.' Softly, not looking up.

'Is that your apology? Don't put me down again, Sandy, in front of anyone, and don't ever invade my privacy. I mean it.'

'I won't.'

'Otherwise you can mop your own floors. In fact, stay away from me.'

Sandy turned to glance at her.

Men, she knew, invested more than they'd admit. 'You look terrible,' she said. 'I'll make coffee. How strong do you need it?'

So Renee and Sandy called a truce, and Renee kept going. When it snowed, she suggested that Dwayne drive his Drift Dipper over and then spread the word: clear access to the lake from the Jacksona.

She left the local paper lying around, then on Sunday she brought in the fat one from the Cities. One day she cleaned Sandy's office and found files piled on his desk, the top one labeled 'Property Insurance', with a note. 'Due February. Pay early.' Was he trying to be more organized? She left the bottle of brandy on the floor, but the next time she went to the laundromat, she took his sleeping bag from off his couch.

Renee designed a new look: she dug out the black, bibbed apron with 'Oscars' stitched across the top and she wore it over her jeans and sweaters, tied tight in front to give herself a waist. It reminded her how far she'd come.

She invented scratch soup. Scratched around for inexpensive ingredients at the grocery store and tried different versions.

'Made from scratch,' she said to Zac as she set the slow cooker on the bar.

Zac had just introduced himself as Jerry's cousin. He came up every season, to get away from the Cities.

He smiled when he told her, 'My folks brought old Jerry up here years ago, and he liked it right away.'

It was warm in the bar and he pulled his stocking cap off. Renee looked at his hands — his line of work? Something soft that paid for a house in the suburbs.

'Ya, then we spent some time here when he came back from Nam.'

'How was he then?'

'Not great. Going through the motions.'

'Was he married?'

'Ya, but it was before Michael was born. A long time before.'

She slotted in this information and handed him a full bowl and a spoon.

'Do you know about the accident with his elbow?'

'I'm not even sure it was an accident, but Jerry's not a talker. Anyway, who'd want to resurrect that?'

'Tell me about this place, Zac.' Because he was a man who wasn't afraid of words and would talk.

'Cross Lake? Ten miles of unruliness. I like that. Like the cowboys who live here. But Sandy's an outlaw. He's run a few schemes in his time. Ever hear the story about the walleye pike flown in from Canada?'

She shook her head. 'He wasn't in Vietnam, was he?'

'He disappeared for a while; that's a fact. Whether you think that was right or wrong, I can't say. But he opened this place up again and it's still standing after all these years.'

'Like the Bachelors. Still standing.' She picked up the ladle, but he put his hand over his bowl.

'Jerry's mentioned the work you've done on him, Renee. He needs somebody to show him the difference between surviving and living.' Zac looked her in the eye. 'Jerry moves slow. A nudge wouldn't hurt. Had many other customers?'

'Some enquiries.'

'Those cards by the cash register – you have to actually give them away. And anybody mention when the new local directory's coming out?'

She had a flash: surrounded by men, but not enough respect from them. She wanted to tell him that it was hard all by herself. She said, 'I don't think we're supposed to sell food. So I just have an honesty jar.'

'What's that?'

'Please leave some money, whatever it's worth.'

Dusk was a frozen mist on top of the lake.

That's what Jerry saw when he woke up on the camp bed and staggered to the fish house door. The brandy laced with coffee that Sandy had poured was high-test. Had given him pseudo courage to take up the challenge: how long could you lie on the ice in Sven's coat, rolling around like a seal? Sandy holding a stopwatch, shouting, 'Come on inside. This ain't fun without an audience.' And Jerry had a hell of a time getting up, Sandy not making a move to help.

Now Jerry's arm hurt all the way past his shoulder. His chest hurt. He'd better not tell Renee. It was eerie outside – no cars, no machinery noise. Everyone gone, the lucky ones to clean fish.

The mist had shifted and the sun going down made it easier to see, on the horizon, a black 4x4 truck. He watched headlights coming closer and soon heard the wind whipping along the ice, accompanying the engine.

'Rescue Squad!' Words shouted out the driver's window, and the headlights blazing.

Jerry recognized Zac's voice and walked out to meet him. 'Hey Zac. Sorry you missed the opening, but we left some fish in the lake for you.' He was happier to see him than he wanted to show. 'New vehicle? You rich businessmen have it made.' Jerry glanced at the empty seat. 'So where is he? He wasn't planning to leave me out here all night?'

Zac said, 'Nothing biting. Sandy's a bad loser.'

Jerry had seen it all before. Sandy wizened, small-minded, sportsmanship a dirty word. He said, 'Bring back the spear. We'd have more luck.'

'Sandy wants to talk business. Let's hear what he's got to say. Dinner's on me tonight. And let's invite your bartender. Does she like steak?'

'She likes pain.'

'What?' Zac grinned.

'She does acupuncture.' He could say the word without flinching, get all the syllables in the correct order. What he wouldn't say: early last week, she'd talked him into signing a consent form. Then later he'd felt a tingling near his elbow because, without warning, she'd used a needle. Like a man, she'd slipped it in.

Renee appreciated the invitation, drove herself to the run-down steakhouse near Loon Mission. Sandy was busy writing a list on his paper napkin. Jerry ordered steak in mushroom sauce which might be easier to cut. Zac, the perfect host, asked Renee about her business.

She told them about the lady in Lakeville whose husband had slipped on the front stoop, wrenched his knee, didn't like the doctor. Would Renee drive over and talk to him? Tomorrow morning. Zac raised his glass to hers and Renee said her White Russian was delicious and Sandy muttered it was because someone else mixed it.

Zac ignored that, remarked that the Jacksona had been cleaned up a hell of a lot. With summer coming, they could make some decent money.

Renee watched the men's attention slide to the waitress in her fluffy sweater as she set down plates. Except for Jerry, who was looking at her. Then he looked over Sandy's shoulder to read aloud: 'repairs, restaurant, outside toilet block, beach for kids—'

'Let's eat first.' Sandy was brusque and Renee understood that he didn't want her there, didn't want to talk in front of her. Shy or embarrassed? His usual moody mixture.

'Well, I can't stay long,' Renee said. 'I really want this new client and I need to phone him at eight on the dot.'

That's how she handled that.

And the next day the visit went well. Renee made a lot of eye contact with the husband, was gentle with her questions. She wanted him to think it over; he called that afternoon to make an appointment. She wanted to celebrate but she was by herself.

It snowed beautifully that night and she got off the couch and walked down to the lake. If there was a time to reach out and wish for someone to share with, this was one of those times. She saw herself for who she was. A woman who'd been alone for a long time. Who'd learned the hard way that if you give yourself away to men when you're young, you empty out. And the only way to change was to fill yourself up again.

Zac's phrase had stayed on her mind. What was the difference between surviving and living? It was love, or connection. However you defined it.

Winter passed as they waited for the heaves of ice to melt and the dirty snow to shrink into pools of coffee-colored water. Jerry took her out to the fish house, let her walk around, then sit inside on a folding chair and stare into the fishing holes, iced over and remote. She saw men who needed to push against the elements.

Jerry said, 'Season's over. Moving back to shore. We had our fun.'

'Well, I'm glad I saw it.'

He said, 'What do you want to do now?'

And she laughed. The thaw had definitely begun.

They drove to Onamia. She showed him where the woman with the headaches lived, client number two. Who'd opened the door and talked for half an hour straight.

They ate wood-fired pizza at the bar next to the pawn shop and Jerry sat beside her so they both had the view. Sun on ice, still enough snow to blur the line between shore and lake.

'Jerry, how's your arm? What about another session?'

'Who's asking? The acupuncturist or—'

They stared at the lake: blurred boundaries, which she was about to trespass.

'Or your girlfriend,' Renee added.

'Show me,' Jerry answered, and she kissed him. 'Should I sign a consent form?' But his eyes were crinkled: he was smiling from inside, a rare sight.

She went to Jerry's trailer the following day. She went for comfort because she knew she could. So he shared his canned ravioli, added onion and a shriveled pepper and it wasn't bad. She'd gotten up from her chair and sat on his lap and kissed him some more; then he turned on his electric blanket. She wouldn't take off anything except her boots. Like an old cowboy, he'd laughed, and they lay under the duvet and she whispered that his bed was as warm as oatmeal.

He'd touched her where she wanted to be touched, the light dusky when she awoke.

Now he was walking over to turn on the heater and blue lights. 'Good thing we left the dishes on the table. Almost time for supper.'

'I should go.'

'The small and the brave.' Jerry shrugged. 'We're not kids anymore.'

'I know,' she said. 'But this is Bachelors Road.'

'So what if they see your car?'

'We're in this together, aren't we?'

'You make it sound like a big hole.' He looked at her carefully.

'I like it here, Jerry, and I like you.'

Those were days she had to tread carefully, all the time reassuring herself that her love life was her business, wasn't it? The men would find out soon enough about her and Jerry; she couldn't worry about it.

Sandy was cold, his mind snapped shut, in a wintry place where nothing could meld into anything else. The air behind his office door stale menthol.

The March weather had turned, the Bachelors trading their parkas for padded sweatshirts. Zac was up for a few days; he and Sandy and Jerry drove off in Jerry's truck, returned with a pool table and the story of how at the gas station Sandy slipped into the driver's seat and took off, leaving Jerry holding three bottles of neon orange pop. But they'd come back with an idea.

'Prohibition party,' Sandy announced. 'I mean near the end of Prohibition. We researched it on Zac's laptop. A law in April 1933 allowed beer and wine. Listen to this: 'THE JACKSONA – STILL STANDING AFTER ALL THESE YEARS'. Zac's slogan. We'll put an ad in the paper. What are you staring at?' he asked her. 'Don't you think we can pull this off?'

Cold for weeks, this was infinitely better. 'Yes, I'm impressed.'

'We'll buy lasagne from the discount. And fix the dock. That'll be Jerry's job.'

'What about me?' Renee asked.

'Can you design some matchbooks? A little phillumeny. And invent an illegal cocktail. Something cheap that tastes expensive.' He turned away. 'Jerry, my man. We need more women. Invite your wife. Tell her to bring her friends.'

In bed she asked Jerry if he'd told Sandy about them.

'What do you think? No.'

'So why did he say that about your wife?'

'He's stirring it up.'

'Why aren't you divorced?'

'I never think about it, I'd rather think about Sandy's dock.'

'You're changing the subject.'

'There's no subject, Renee. Edie May stays away. She

84

tells me when Michael's in town. That's it.'

'Edie May? What kind of name is that?'

'Drop it.'

She'd have to accept that and trust him. Otherwise, what was she doing here? There were other things to accept also: these men were bound together by the lake and what they'd survived, and did not always play by the rules.

'What's that smell?' Jerry wanted to know, walking into Renee's kitchen.

'Dinner.'

'No, the other one.'

'Incense.'

'Put it out,' and because he'd spat out the words, she did.

He'd stayed rough and abrupt for two hours, loosened up when they walked down to the lake where she asked, 'What does the incense remind you of, Jerry?'

He'd stared straight ahead. 'They were always starting fires in Nam, the place was burning up, smoke and rice and dead animals. There was this sweet smell that made me retch.'

'Animals?'

'Sometimes they rolled cigarettes in salt and fed them to the deer.'

Renee knew there was more, women and children and burning huts.

'Have to live with it. Doesn't help to spread it around.' Jerry started walking away.

She thought: Those Vietnamese women didn't stand a chance.

That night she lay in her bed with her face against his back. She told him about the other soldier in her life. Her senior year and she was impatient with those high school boys fumbling around inside the old Jameson Factory. Ken was the older guy who'd drifted around town, as if waiting for Renee to walk by in that tight black skirt.

He was the only person she really knew who'd been to Vietnam. He was old, in his thirties, and one day let it slip that he'd been an officer, but that was a decade ago, didn't mean anything now. He was just trying to get back to normal life and she didn't understand really, but liked the attention. And he only brought her to his apartment once and there was nothing out of place, except for the bathrobe on the back of the door which was his sister's. After that, he carried a sleeping bag in his car and some of the rum she liked.

Then one night he wanted to take some pictures. He'd brought his camera. He wanted the shape and the smell of her. Would she give him that bra and her underpants?

The next week she'd found herself in a motel room on the cheap side of town where the sheets weren't very clean and his ideas of what to do on them were not either.

At school a teacher had stopped her in the corridor. 'Renee, did you forget about the college entrance meeting?'

She'd forgotten a lot of things that year.

Now she said, 'I always wondered what he did with my underwear.'

Jerry grunted softly. 'There was a lot of that going down.'

'What do you mean?'

'Money. Bets. What could you talk your wife into sending? They'd hang it on a wall. One side for wives, one for whores.'

Renee lay still.

'There were a lot of contests.'

'Were there?'

'Look. The officers were under pressure, we all were. We did regrettable things.'

'Your arm? It wasn't an accident, was it?'

'Nothing about that war was clear-cut.' He turned onto his back. 'Doesn't help to go over it.'

'I'm trying to understand.'

'You can't.'

The next morning Jerry told her that this was the first place where he could actually fall asleep without facing the door. He liked that cold wall that faced outside. He was closer to the lake.

The Prohibition party gave them hope for the summer ahead. The April evening warm enough to have the doors propped open, an idea that passing cars might see and stop. Some did. The coupon in the paper for the half-price cocktail helped.

The evening came together. Sandy, proud of the place. Renee, in a long red dress, behind the bar, handing out matchbooks like party favors. Diane and Steve, from the wedding last October, wandered in, grinning. The lake was calm: cooperative. Jerry made sure the half dozen customers who'd come over in their motorboats had help tying up. When he came inside, he told Renee the ground smelled of moss and fishbones, and she pictured him with his hands in his pockets, inhaling something new.

Sandy dragged a chair over to the bar near Renee, turned the CD player off, clapped his hands while he climbed up on the chair.

'I just want to say', he began and then swallowed, awkward now that he had his customers' attention. 'Hey, this is a really good start to the season. I sure hope so. Thanks for coming. Keep coming back, guys – and thanks to Renee and Jerry for helping me out. That's it.'

He grinned sheepishly when they applauded and then someone turned the music back on.

Renee said, 'Just right, Sandy. Sven would have liked it.'

His face was gentle with pleasure. 'I bought you a present. It's in my office. Come on.'

She followed him because she didn't want to ruin anything. When he turned on the light she saw a soft mint green sweatshirt, fitted, with a hood. Expensive.

'Just take it,' and his voice was gruff.

'It's too nice.' Renee heard the words come out: 'I'm with Jerry now.'

He looked at her and laughed. 'Nothing lasts forever, sweetheart. Wear it,' he said, 'when nights are cold.'

The Bachelors were out on the lake in Sandy's boat, staying alert for the smoke spiral which would materialize into the first hatch of mayflies. Brown, strange flies that sat on windscreens, side mirrors. You closed your doors and windows against their low hum. The flies were late this year.

How the lake welcomed the men back, gently rocked Sandy's boat. Steele had completely overhauled Sandy's motor, all winter working in his kitchen, an old tent covering the floor.

They'd teased him the way he'd slept with that outboard. At least she was better than his last girlfriend, they laughed. Because Steele had a way of finding women who used him.

'Oh ya,' Steele said. 'So how's *your* girlfriend, Jerry?'

Sandy trailed his hand in the water. Played dumb.

Jerry was experimenting with his fishing reel, letting out line. 'Which girlfriend is that?'

'I've seen you together,' Steele nodded. 'She's always talking to you.'

'She likes to talk. Likes it up here.'

Steele opened the cooler and passed around beers. 'If she can handle you walking around in your underwear, I guess the mayflies won't scare her.'

They twisted the caps off simultaneously, lifted the bottles to their lips. End of conversation.

Her phone was ringing and it woke her. She hadn't meant to leave it on: last night was a late night at the bar.

'Renee?'

'Jerry. What time is it?'

'Seven. Beautiful day. Here's what I'm thinking. I want to show you the place where the old drive-in theater used to be. Where we buried the time capsule.'

'Who?'

'Me and Zac. Let's dig it up.'

Renee smiled: the child not completely gone.

Some days are fresh and waiting for us. That's what Renee thought when Jerry walked in her back door an hour later with an armful of rhubarb which grew at the back of his trailer.

He had a map, hand-drawn, which he was shy about showing. 'Do you remember that Zac's family first brought me up here, and his dad took us to this drive-in?'

'When you were kids.'

'So Zac and I came back and explored when we hunted up here.' He paused. 'I was just home from Nam. Guess he thought it would bring back good memories.'

In the truck, as he drove to the south side of the lake and the farms outside of Garrison, she stared at the pencil drawing, how he'd gone over it in ballpoint, made the drive-in screen darker, sketched cars in front. She counted twenty-two tiny footprints from the screen to a rectangle marked with an X.

'What is that?'

'The old popcorn stand. And the arrow points to the time capsule. A mayonnaise jar. That's all we had.'

Jerry parked near the first farm, carried a shovel and wore a backpack containing water and Fig Newtons and gave her a light blanket to carry. They were on the edge of a cornfield and climbed over a fence he didn't recognize. He counted to twenty-two as they walked, dug with concentration, was silent, looked lost.

He said, 'I think this map is wrong,' and they both laughed. They sat on the blanket for awhile before he walked off and came back and asked her to follow.

The foot-high section of concrete foundation and a pile of bricks on the vacant ground – all that was left of the refreshments stand. He lifted up a plank of wood, streaked with faded red paint. The bricks had been arranged in a square and covered over with weeds and, when Jerry reached into the space, he unearthed the metal speaker that they'd found and then hid, a few inches of curly cord still attached. He handed it to Renee. 'Remember how this clipped onto the driver's window. It was so loud.'

'I don't remember, Jerry, because drive-ins were before my time.'

'Oh ya, I guess so.'

'When, exactly?'

'It must have been '69. Of course, the drive-in was gone, this big farm bought the land. But we found the speaker right here, made a time capsule, buried it like kids playing pirates, and then we went hunting. Crazy.'

'Was it?'

'Ya, me with a gun.'

'What happened?'

'Nothing bad. Zac kept a close eye.'

She cradled the metal in her hand as if it were treasure. But the real gift: their talking had shifted and gone deeper.

'What about the time capsule, Jerry? Do you want to keep digging?'

'No, I'll talk to Zac. His memory might be better.'

'Maybe he dug it up and didn't tell you? Like a real pirate.'

Jerry stared at her. 'That is bad. That would not happen.'

'Just seeing how far trust goes.' And she poked him in the ribs, making a point.

Jerry was making Renee a gift. It had been a long time since he'd planned a surprise.

He sat at the table in his trailer, wiping his penknife down his shirt. He'd soaked that empty rum bottle and removed the label. Let it dry. Bought a big box of household matches and used his knife to spread glue; now the pirate on the box grinned mischievously back at him.

He rubbed the back of his neck. Too long bent over.

But half of him was somewhere else. For one spectacular moment he was back in Nam with his penknife tucked into his belt. How they cleaned out wounds gritted with dirt. A few seconds of pain and blood made a clean cut, and then the superglue they'd been issued with to close it up: 'Use flat side of knife to apply. Do not allow fingers to come into contact with glue. Wipe blade with clean rag.'

They'd laughed at the invention of superglue for their war, joked about the notion of a clean rag in the jungle. Some nights they joked and went too far and one night they were out to get that smart ass from Georgia, who woke up with his thumb glued to his penis. Now what had he done to deserve that?

A long time ago, Jerry thought, but once in a while, not long enough.

When Renee walked into Jerry's trailer, he handed her a mug of hot chocolate and then poured a capful of rum into it.

'Smugglers Poison,' he told her. 'Invented by Zac. We were twelve when we smuggled his parents' rum out of the cabinet.'

'Your pirate stories. I love them.'

When he handed her the pirate matchbox, it took her thirty seconds to pull it together: the night he'd put on the storm door, he'd taken the empty bottle home.

Jerry sat down in his chair. 'Know what it is?'

'You made this. I can't believe it.'

'Why not? Start a collection.'

'Phillumeny.'

'Ya, big word.'

'Thank you. I just didn't think you'd remember something like that.'

'Why not? We've all heard your boss's sad stories.'

Renee sipped her hot chocolate, then sat on Jerry's

lap and buried her cheek in his shirt. 'I want to be an honorary pirate.' She could feel him laugh. 'Tell me what's in the mayonnaise jar.'

'Nope. Doesn't work like that.'

'The thing about treasure is you don't want it buried so deep you can't find it.'

'What are you saying, Renee?'

'Strong feelings are like treasure.'

'If you say so.'

Renee stayed quiet. This was as close to romance as he could go.

The Bachelors stalked around with bravado through mayflies that swirled and hummed, spent themselves, and dropped softly dead.

Renee parked right outside the Jacksona, rushed in and demanded: 'Is this the plague? Are we being punished for something bad we've done?'

'Not yet,' Jerry said.

'Shut up,' Sandy told him.

'What does that mean, Jerry? Why are you two arguing?'

Sandy smiled at her. 'It's nothing, sweetheart. They'll be gone in a week.'

For days she swept flies off the doors, off her car; she swept all the floors. The fish weren't biting; they were gorging on flies. But that didn't stop the Bachelors from going out each night and trying their luck.

It seemed wrong, Sandy's assumption that she'd work all week by herself.

The third night he said, 'Can you lock up? Dwayne and I are taking Jerry out to the mudflats. You're not the only one who makes that old man happy.' Grabbing his windbreaker and pack of Salems on his way out.

She felt like the hired help. She felt like shouting: *I thought you only smoked in the winter. You'll get cancer.*

And what did they talk about out there for two, three hours? It was a low point. A cold May night, and the few customers left early.

Now Renee poured herself a vodka, mixed in orange juice. This was definitely against her rules, but maybe it wasn't a bad idea to take the edge off so she didn't take this personally, not like when the Bachelors went ice fishing. She sipped her drink and felt better. This was how men behaved up here; nobody owed her an explanation.

Late that night she woke in her housette to a tap on the bedroom window.

Jerry left his jacket and jeans on the floor next to her bed and then sat down. She climbed back in, waited and finally whispered, 'Do you want to talk?'

'Sandy's getting on my nerves. He's too restless for his own good. I'm tired of his voice, tired of flies. He thinks he's always right, but we almost got lost out there in his boat. It was dark as the fucking jungle and no place to run.'

'I'm glad you came over.'

'I'm just an old vet, Renee, trying to get by. I don't want anybody to get hurt.'

'Jerry, if you needed to confide in me, could you do that?'

'Don't know. Maybe.'

They slept until he had one of his dreams at a God-forsaken hour, where he flung his arm out, muttering phrases she was afraid to understand. Leaving his brain sour, hungover; that's what he told her in the morning.

As he stood at her sink, drinking water straight from the faucet, not bothering to cup it in his hands.

'What about a shower?' But he shook his head. She served him coffee and offered: 'Some acupuncture, Jerry. We haven't scheduled any, but it could help.'

He answered, 'You know how to find real customers now, don't you?'

Her stomach sank with familiar disappointment. He'd given her something, now he'd taken something away. How ragged this month was.

The flies vanished and the June sky looked bluer. She felt lighter. Nothing was impossible.

Renee wanted her screens back on her doors, a swimsuit so she could make friends with the lake, a cold tomato-soup recipe, fireworks for the Fourth of July, and fireworks in bed.

When Jerry came over to put her screen door back on, she said, 'Now what can I do for you?'

'You can start by getting rid of that old sweater.'

Summer had begun.

She walked, looking at pale wild iris and ferns, mangled and lush. From the woods she brought back branches with buds peeking open, which she put in jars on the floor, and she found a watering can down at the boathouse and arranged branches for the Jacksona.

She spent money putting an ad in the local paper, then put more business cards on boards in the café, the liquor store and at the Thrift Shop where she'd bought a few things and conversed with the owner, who suffered with leg cramps for no apparent reason.

The owner was named Cherise and had recently added a rail of imperfect outlet store garments and

Renee had immediately loved the robin's-egg blue retro swimsuit.

'You'll see it soon enough,' she told Jerry, 'when we go swimming. I was thinking,' she paused, 'that color blue would look great in the bar.'

Jerry yawned. 'Too far, Renee. Don't get carried away.'

'Why not? It wouldn't cost much.'

'Sandy's not interested in new paint.'

'Not even for the boathouse? It needs the letters repainted. Nobody can read 'JACKSONA' from the lake.'

'Are you talking to me?'

'You did a nice job fixing up the dock.'

Jerry looked her in the eye. 'You got any other ideas?'

'Sure I do. Let me show you.'

Renee gave the Bachelors summer haircuts. Jerry first on a chair outside his trailer. And when he walked into the Jacksona, with hair neatly trimmed and mustache twirled to match, they all wanted a new look, for free. Steele wanted exactly the same and Dwayne kept his cropped, but she neatened it up.

Sandy next. Half an inch, he insisted. Renee could see that Sandy had put in something like 'Nice and Easy' color, though he claimed it was the sun. She knew he was hanging on to what he had left, so she had to take care or he'd never forgive her.

Sandy asked, 'Hey, Jerry, you put Renee's screens on for her yet?'

Renee replied, 'Yes, two weeks ago. But I was thinking that we could have screens on the bar windows. Keep the mosquitoes out. And the porch only has one torn screen that I can see. Can we mend it?'

'I don't know,' Sandy said, but she had her hand on his shoulder as she cut. Captive audience.

'Fourth of July is around the corner. Let's put the pool table out there.'

'I'm not competing with Freddy's; they do the biggest shindig around.'

'Let them,' she said, 'we can be low-key, but we'll need fireworks.'

And the next day the Bachelors walked in with an armload. Sparklers, of course, Cats Eyes, Blood Singers, Star Farters, and something terrible that was only legal in Texas called Ricky's Revenge. The directions warned that it was a slow starter with a long fuse, but then Ricky would keep going for five.

Sandy couldn't say that with a straight face. 'Renee, remind you of anyone you know?'

She gave it back to him. Said that she'd invite her new friend Cherise over, though she was definitely out of Sandy's league.

Steele and Dwayne stamped their feet.

Anyway, who was going to stay sober, Renee wanted to know, besides her. Somebody had to be in charge of the fireworks. The last thing they wanted was an accident.

The Fourth arrived, beautiful and warm.

Renee found Jerry out front near the dock, clearing weeds and dead crayfish from the shore. His jeans legs were pushed up toward his knees; he stood ankle-deep in water. She went inside and came back in her polka dot swimsuit.

His wolf whistle cut the air. 'Going in?'

'I'm waiting for you.'

'I'm not much of a swimmer, Renee.'

'Neither am I. That's why I need you.' She was pacing the shore to let her feet get wet. Over her shoulder she said, 'Sandy's car isn't here.'

'Nope.'

'Yesterday a guy turned up and wanted Sandy to take him and his girlfriend out for a ride. Sandy told him his boat was in storage, but it's right there in your boat harbor. All he'd have to do is bring it around The Point.'

'Back to being lazy. But today his curiosity got the better of him and he drove over to Freddy's.'

When Cherise arrived, Renee looked at the scene through the other woman's eyes: three older men dunking beef jerky strips in their glasses of beer. Cherise stood in the doorway wearing a skirt made out of cotton handkerchiefs, carrying a cake pan, dangling her car key.

'I made it. Hello.' Bold and confident, she was a breath of fresh air.

'Come in. Let me introduce you to the guys.'

'Have I missed Happy Hour?'

'Hell, no,' Sandy said. 'It's Happy Day. Beer's only a buck.' He ran his hand through his hair, then reached out to shake hers. Jerry grinned and tipped his baseball hat. Steele glanced up from his newspaper. Dwayne had somewhere else to be.

'Cherise owns the new Thrift Shop in Lakeville. You all need to stop in there, never know what you might find.'

'That's true. Renee, I've been trawling so many garage sales. I've brought you a present in my car. Now don't let me forget it. And for the rest of you, I just happen to have my card.' She reached into her purse. 'Maybe I could leave a few,' she said to Sandy. 'Small businesses need to support each other. May I have yours?'

'I'm working on that,' Sandy said, and Steele chuckled.

She'd turned to Steele. 'And what do you do?'

'Nothing.'

'He fishes,' Jerry said, 'and does maintenance on our boats.'

'This is a great spot, needs a few boats out front. What brings in your customers? Cheap beers before eight?'

'Seven,' Sandy corrected her.

'So what rhymes with seven? Renee, we need some paper.'

In ten minutes, a card was designed:

'Go to Heaven Before 7
Happy Hour Beer $2.00
The Jacksona, on the East Side.'

'Let's put Jacksona,' Renee said, 'in capital letters to match the boathouse. We still might get around to re-painting them.'

'A phone number is important,' Cherise said, 'and an old landline would look great on the bar as a feature. Nostalgia. That's what you're selling here.'

When Cherise mentioned driving over to Freddy's, Sandy shook his head. She stared at the three men glued to their bar stools. The women took a walk, made coffee, served rhubarb cake. It eased into evening.

'Well, this is our own private party,' Cherise said. 'I like it.'

Sandy, Renee noticed, stayed sober for the fireworks on the beach. Although afterwards he made up for it, telling Renee not to be so stingy with his liquor.

When Cherise said she was hungry, Sandy went in the kitchen and made grilled ham and cheese. Steele couldn't take his eyes off their guest, cheese oozing out of his sandwich.

Renee's lasting impressions: mustard on Jerry's mustache, which she kissed off, and Cherise, holding a lighted sparkler, twirling in her handkerchief skirt, on the checkered linoleum floor.

The pale pink shoe box. Renee waited until the next day to try on the shoes. 'I hope they fit,' Cherise had said when Renee walked her to her car. 'If they're tight, push hot sponges into the toes.'

The shoes were brown, velvety, not too high, and they shaped her calves and her attitude the minute she slipped them on. What she loved best was the red tulip sewn onto the back seam of each shoe. Like a secret not everyone would share, only when she walked away.

She was going to wear those shoes for Jerry. Barelegged; in the long red dress from the Prohibition party one moonlit night out on the grass.

What was it that Cherise had whispered when she'd climbed into her car? 'Jerry's a little withdrawn, isn't he? Is this going anywhere?'

'He's hard to get to know and I don't want to wreck anything.'

'I see. You're riding the day-to-day because you want the steamy nights.'

'Come to Onamia with me. I've had a referral.'

Jerry looked at her.

'Do you remember the older man who fell down on

his sidewalk, who took a while to warm up to me?'

Jerry grunted.

'His wife called. She wants me to meet her son-in-law who's having a bad time at work. Come with me. We haven't been to Onamia for months.'

Renee studied his face to see if he remembered sitting next to her, shoulders touching, that first kiss.

'I know this is unusual, but the guy asked if he could meet another client. I really want this job. Would you tell him about my work on your arm?'

'What do you want me to say?' Then he lowered his voice, just for her. 'I'm not good at that stuff, Renee. You know that.'

'Let's see how this goes. Try.'

Driving back from Onamia, Renee felt that the appointment had gone better than she'd expected. The woman had taken them for a walk around her garden, so dull last winter and now full of brown-eyed Susans. Her son-in-law joined them in the garden and the conversation had been informal but constructive.

In the car she thanked Jerry for his help. She felt relieved, relaxed, was talking more than usual.

Jerry was listening, but it turned out that he was listening to her car engine.

'Why? What's wrong with it?'

'Probably needs oil. Don't worry. I've got some in my shed.'

Harmony and energy: she wanted to continue. Renee wanted to work on Jerry's shoulder; Jerry wanted to work on sex.

Renee laughed but she could see the connection:

everything interesting between them happened in bed or on her couch.

'I'd like you on the treatment table, please. Let's do this right.'

'I'm not feeling bad.'

'You could feel even better. Don't you trust me?'

She would use the point called Gate of Hope, and she wished for him openness in his heart and for his future. She realized it was risky, being involved with someone she was treating. But she also couldn't convince herself that his days of fruitful work and real commitment were completely gone. So she offered Jerry a chance to rebalance his Fire and strengthen his Water Element. More joy, less fear.

And he surrendered for two sessions: no needle jokes, no interruptions, just acupuncturist and client in quiet morning sun.

It was time for the red dress. Between the twilight moon and her brown velvet shoes, he wouldn't stand a chance. Two kitchen chairs set out by the tree in the back and an ice bucket filled with glasses and a bottle; a blanket on the sparse grass.

She wouldn't let him near her until she'd had a glass of wine and kicked off her shoes. She told him she wasn't wearing any underwear, lured him down to the blanket and if he was a bit rough, she liked it.

Afterwards, he refused to stay outside. Mosquitoes – and somebody might drive by. When he stood up, she thought about how seldom she'd seen him naked; most of the time they were wrapped together in the dark.

In her bed he didn't pull away and kissed her more than once. She touched his chest, the place where she lay her hand when they talked late at night.

'Was it nice for you?'

'It was different, but I'm not into games. You're not playing with me, are you, Renee?'

If she closed her eyes, would he tell her more?

'In the army we played games and forgot to stop. One time we talked about which soldier you wanted with you if you got cut down. Then carved his initials on our—'

'Jerry. You've paid for this already.'

He turned toward the door.

She kissed his back and whispered, 'You deserve to be happy. That's what I want for you.'

The next morning he opened the bathroom door and stared at her in the bathtub. With her smile she invited him in.

'Renee, Sandy needs me to move Steele's boat.'

'Are you always going to do what Sandy wants?'

'When Steele can't fish, he loses it. I have to go.'

Feel free, she almost said, but didn't because they'd never be free. 'I was going to serve your rhubarb on French toast, but I can save it. I just picked it the other day. Why are you looking at me like that? End of season, couldn't waste it.'

He glared at her. 'You were prowling around my trailer?'

'I knocked on your door, you weren't there. What's the big deal?'

'Nothing. Sorry.' Jerry tipped his imaginary hat at her and closed the door.

She knew: an intimate step forward, a fearful half-step back.

For three days, Renee watched him work. The first afternoon, Jerry poured bucket after bucket of lake water onto the dock, scrubbed it with an old broom. He raked the shore and cleaned the birdbath. He scrubbed the boathouse.

Renee let him work, walking out to the porch to make sure he was still wearing a hat, not sunburned, not going into himself too much. Once, she brought him iced coffee, once a jug of water.

The next afternoon, she saw a ladder against the boathouse door. When she walked down there, she found an open can of paint, the skin on top startlingly white like a fresh start. She wondered what size brush he would use for the letters and then thought she might cry. He'd hardly made eye contact; they'd barely talked. Was she losing him? He was near an edge and her job was to let him know that she cared if he came back. She hoped he wore his sturdy boots going up that ladder.

When Sandy came to look for her, Renee was down on her knees, washing the floor of the screened-in porch. The bare boards looked better than that old piece of linoleum.

She had the feeling Sandy had been watching for a while before he said, 'Renee, what's going on?'

'Jerry hosed down the screens. I'm finishing it off.'

'What for?'

'Drinks and popcorn.' She peeled off a rubber glove and smiled. 'When Cherise comes over, you can serve sandwiches. We'll pretend that your hygiene certificates aren't six years out of date. And maybe you could find a new bulb for the ceiling light so nobody trips over and sues us.'

'Hell, the whole place needs rewiring.'

They stayed silent for a moment.

'Where've you been, Sandy?'

'Taking care of a few things. And it looks like you've kept Jerry real busy. How *is* your old man? You two engaged yet?'

'Mind your own business.'

'I'd like to, Renee. I would like to mind my own business. So stop with all this. We just need to make it through the summer.'

'Why? When you can sit out here until October.'

Sandy turned on his heel. 'If you're bringing tables in here, be sure to scrape off all the chewing gum underneath.'

If she answered, it would make things worse.

'Not talking? Well, before you put the ring on your finger, you might ask why his wife's been visiting him up here.'

'I don't believe you.'

'You are beautifully naive, Renee. That's why we love you.'

She would not give him the satisfaction of answering. She finished the floor while he was in his office, and left.

But there was only so long Renee could drive around looking at the lake. She left a message: 'Your wife comes up to visit and you don't tell me?' She felt like a small-town girl with old-fashioned ideas who'd been treating summer romance as if it were the real thing. She cleared her throat. 'What's going on?'

On the phone Jerry said, 'I don't know what Sandy told you, but she's only been here once.'

'What for?'

'One night she wanted to talk.'

Renee laughed.

'Look,' he said. 'I'm not going back there. She don't even want me back. She's a ghost on the road. But I'm not going to throw her out when it's because of her that our kid turned out all right. I guess she's like everybody else, trying to figure out the next move.' He was quiet for a moment. 'You still there, Renee?'

'Yes, I'm here. And you know why? Because I like it here.' With or without you, she thought, and shivered. The afternoon had begun to close down. 'I need a bath. Let me know if you really want to talk.'

He was losing her. She was disappearing. Jerry felt it in his gut but he had to try.

He walked into the Jacksona wearing a clean denim shirt and said he wasn't leaving without her. 'I'll wait on the porch.' When she brought him a beer, he said, 'The way those screens were slapped up, hit and miss. But the view is worth it.'

'I need ten minutes.'

'Just tell him you're going.'

In Loon Mission they sat quietly on their bar stools, legs not touching. He told her that he'd let it out about Edie May one night when he and Sandy were drinking.

'Jerry. You don't talk to me for three days, and then I hear this from him?' She sighed. 'You should have told me first, then he couldn't have used it for ammunition. Can you see that?'

He nodded, looked away. He couldn't get it out of his mind. The red dress morning Sandy had tricked him into driving to the boat harbor and then blurted it out: he was cutting his losses and letting the bar go. If Jerry wanted to help, there might be some money. Insurance money.

Renee pushed her hair behind her ears. 'Jerry, don't

look so sad. It's okay.'

'Is it?' Because he'd pushed Sandy backward, hard, by the shoulders, his gut reaction that he'd become involved when he didn't want to be, couldn't afford to be. And Sandy, white-lipped, had smiled: 'You're just worried that Renee might not stick around if she doesn't have the Jacksona. Doesn't say much for you then, does it?'

'Jerry?' Renee said.

He forced himself to look up. 'I wasn't sure how you'd take it.'

'Now you know.' Her eyes were searching his face. 'Take me swimming. The water's not going to get any warmer.'

Jerry kept the motor low as he steered Sandy's boat out of the harbor to the dock where Renee stood with a towel around her waist and a red scarf around her hair, looking out at crashing waves. A boat ride would clear his head.

'Come on,' he said.

'No, I want to feel the sand and the weeds.'

He was staring at her because she'd still look good in ten years, though he wouldn't be around to see.

And then she stopped waiting for him. She slipped out of the towel and backed down the ladder that no one used. She was in up to her shoulders, and the whitecaps grew as she pulled off her red scarf and walked into the wave that came straight for her.

Sandy phoned, and in his huskiest, saddest voice said, 'Renee, there's been a fire.'

'What do you mean?' Her stomach plummeting.

'The Jacksona. Don't drive over. It looks worse than it is.'

'Was it the kitchen?'

'The fire department's been and gone. We're taking care of it. Call you later.'

'Wait.' She stood, unwanted on men's territory. 'When did it happen?'

'Late. Don't know exactly. I was home having a beer with the neighbor.'

She smelled it before she saw it. Red and white security tape had been pulled across the parking lot entrance. She parked on the highway and pressed the heels of her hands against her eyes. She would not cry here. A few cars went by and people stared. The blue and white sheriff's car drove slowly by.

The building had not burned down to the ground because of the four-foot wall of bricks. As much permanence as Sven could afford. Renee saw charred plasterboard and the remains of the roof, a burned rafter that had fallen into the restaurant. Somebody had dragged the pool table outside, and one of the porch screens had been thrown onto the ground out front. She could see the stainless steel counter in the kitchen and the refrigerator blackened with soot. She couldn't look at the long wooden bar. All the years and all the varnish.

If her world was not exactly turned inside out, her heart was.

She knocked once on the trailer door and called his name and then walked in. She could not read him, lying on his bed watching the silent television, barefoot. Once they'd soaked their feet in buckets of sugar water. It was like everything they'd done together, beginnings of good habits, but not enough.

She said, 'I cried in the car so I don't cry here. It's a mess over there.'

She'd been shivering; now she was hot. She stripped off her sweatshirt and dropped it on the floor. 'This is the worst part. Seeing you. I don't really care about your version.'

'Are you going to hear me out, Renee?'

'You knew he was up to something. All his talk about surviving the summer.'

'That was weeks ago. I thought he'd dropped it.'

'Sandy can't keep his schemes to himself. He needs you Bachelors to back him up.'

'I didn't back him up. I wanted you to stay the innocent party. In case anything went wrong.'

She stared at the floor, saw his moccasins under the table. The duct tape on one hanging on. Like her.

'You should have told me. I could have talked to him.'

'He wouldn't take that. He would have figured out something worse.' They stared at each other for a minute. 'He could hurt you, Renee.'

'I am hurt.' You learn, she thought, to act like a woman with backbone, instead of a bartender in the middle of nowhere. 'Don't call and don't come over.'

FORGIVENESS BY ANOTHER NAME, 2008

Edie May stared at falling leaves out the picture window. She was working up to phoning her son Michael who lived in Everglades City and this was not going to be as easy as usual.

The October weather was preparing to turn and she wondered what kind of weather he had down in Florida. It could get cold, he'd told her, but wouldn't last. As for her, she never knew what kind of winter they were in for. It could last forever, or at least until March.

Which is what had happened two and a half years ago when Michael was deployed from Iraq and came to stay in her house in Cambridge that she'd then owned for a year. When a freak snowstorm blew in from Canada, he'd volunteered to shovel the sidewalk and driveway, throw sand down so she wouldn't slip. She'd watched from the front window though she tried not to – the more privacy she gave him, the longer he might stay – and saw him rub sand over one cheek and his chin, then turn his face to the sky. When he walked into the kitchen he said, 'Those sunglasses you sent me, they saved my ass. Sometimes that sand ripped into our faces; you wouldn't believe the desert.' Then he smiled at her. 'I saw you watching, Mom. Had to feel the difference between sand and snow.'

She loved that part of him. He'd always talked to her, even as a teenager, and he'd written her short letters from Iraq and phoned when he could. She knew it was partly because he didn't have a girlfriend to take up his time, and she'd been selfishly grateful for that, though deep down she worried that he'd broken up with a nice teacher before he went overseas; she worried that he'd never been in love since Carla Hoppe.

But she had something more urgent on her mind right now so she was going to call and if he was busy at work, he'd phone her back, but he was never distant. His voice lifted her: it belonged to a twenty-eight-year-old who was handsome and idealistic in spite of her, she sometimes felt, rather than because of any great parenting she and Jerry had done.

Jerry. That's who she needed to tell him about.

At Ted's Old Fishing Shop Michael lifted the black receiver from its old-fashioned cradle and glanced around the room with its quirky interior design: 1950's phone on the counter, Beach Boys poster on the wall next to a display of classic sea fishing reels.

Michael was glad she'd called. 'How's everything?'

'I'm worried about your father. He stopped answering his phone.'

'That's nothing new, Mom.'

'This divorce is never going to happen. My lawyer sent a duplicate set of documents to his PO box and nothing's come back.' She paused. 'I finally got hold of him. He's too busy to collect his mail.'

'Busy doing what?'

'Clearing out his cave. Preparing to hibernate. That's what he said.'

Michael laughed.

'It's not funny. He called yesterday, and demanded we collect your boxes. Or else he'll burn them.'

'The Bachelors will keep an eye on him.'

'They already are.' His mother's voice went quiet. 'They've been on the alert since Jerry tried to shoot the lock off that cabin door.'

'In August? I thought that blew over.'

'The place was empty and nobody pressed charges, if that's what you mean. But Jerry was in a scuffle last week in town. Things haven't settled down. In fact, they're getting worse.'

'Maybe Zac can check in. Dad likes his cousin.'

'I've tried, Michael, but he's tied up. Zac says to phone him when you arrive and give him a report. His advice is: no deer hunting this year.'

Shit, Michael thought.

'I think your father needs you.'

'Really?' Michael said sarcastically, and then sifting through her words, 'Wait a minute. What boxes?'

'Brandy snifters from your Aunt Rebecca, and I saved your yearbooks and photos of Carla.'

'What are you bringing her up for?'

'We went out to lunch. Well, you knew we exchange Christmas cards and now they've moved up to Forest Lake, so she's not far away.'

'She still married to Dougie Schultz?'

'Yes, she is.'

'I have to go.'

'I know,' she said. 'Think it over and call me. Please.'

That evening Michael sat on his sofa with the map on his lap. In his mind he shot through the Cities, past Forest Lake and Cambridge, up to the bigger lakes. When he returned from Iraq, he'd bought this new road atlas, as if it could help him understand his parents' separate lives – his mother in her little house; his father in a trailer on Cross Lake; and him in limbo until he decided on Florida.

Once, he'd calculated all the distances between them, wrote them down in the margin: ancient stuff.

He picked up his landline.

'Michael,' she answered. 'Nice of you to call so soon.'

'You didn't tell me the whole story about Dad shooting that door, did you?'

'I didn't feel like saying it was his girlfriend's rented house. Why would I?'

'Okay, I see your point, but Zac had filled me in anyway. What else?'

'Did Zac tell you I had the phone call from the sheriff's office? Jerry put me down as next of kin and they needed someone to pay the damages. If we could pay up front, they could go easy on him.'

'So you paid up?'

'I couldn't abandon him.'

'You still can't. Don't you think that helping him out with money and then saying you want a divorce is giving him a double message?'

'No, I don't.'

'So what exactly are you asking me to do, Mom?'

'Visit us. Help your father get back on an even keel.'

On the phone his father had been cool when Michael said he was thinking about a trip to see them. 'Time goes fast, Dad,' and Jerry said, 'Does it?' As if *he*, Jerry, were the injured party, Michael thought. *You started this cold front*, he'd wanted to say, *out in my parking lot*. And then there'd been his father's aborted visit to Florida.

It wasn't until he actually stood in front of his old man in his driveway and Jerry said, 'So your mother sent you to take inventory?', his eyes crinkling in the old way and father and son had managed a handshake, that Michael laughed and decided this trip wasn't such a bad idea.

'Your fishing season's finished?' Jerry wanted to know.

'Down there it's never over, but my friend Doobie stepped in to help. He's been working with the boss since he was a kid.'

'Did I meet him?'

'No, but I told you about my army buddy who's a trained guide on the islands, keeps up his license. He's teaching me.'

'You've got a good deal.'

'I work hard. Do the extras, before Ted asks.'

'Ya? Like what?'

'Organize tackle, wash down the slicks, I even clean the toilet.'

When Jerry smirked, Michael reminded him, 'You taught me that, at Al's garage. Remember the filthy sink from using Lava soap?' Without thinking, both men glanced down at their fingernails. 'Al let me hang around and change oil, remember?' Then he filled the pause with: 'The good old days.'

Jerry shrugged. 'So how'd your car run on this trip?'

It had been two and a half years since Michael had met the Bachelors. If they all looked older, well so did he.

'Nice tan,' Dwayne said. 'Florida must be treating you

good. Hope you're staying here longer than last time.'

'Two weeks, spending some of it in Cambridge.'

'Keeping an eye on the folks. Good idea. Maybe you'll have time to work on your dad's truck. We're hoping to run our Ditch Dipper business again. Give Jerry some direction and keep him busy. Since the fire, it's been tough.'

What was it his mother had said? Jerry was manic, clearing out debris, but in the shed tools and tires and lawn mowers had just been moved around or maybe there were more.

Jerry was planning to put the fold-up cot in the corner of the trailer, the way they'd done it when Michael returned from Iraq. He'd only stayed two nights, checking in before moving to Florida, staring unblinkingly at the magnificent lake, sad that his parents had separated – Edie thinner, not taking up enough space in her house, and Jerry up here on weird Bachelors Road.

Now Michael understood that his re-entry into civilian life had happened too fast. He couldn't absorb the changes, could barely remember the names of the Bachelors who'd crawled out of the woods to be introduced, who shook his hand firmly and respectfully without many words.

This time he was genuinely glad to see them; Michael knew they were a safety net.

'What about Sandy?' he asked. 'He still around?'

'Nope,' Dwayne said. 'Not since the clubhouse burned down.'

'I never really heard the full story about that.'

'Don't think anybody has.'

Michael had been there one day and Bachelors Road felt completely different; hadn't changed at all. Both were true.

He liked sitting in Jerry's shed. One old chair and a wooden beer crate for a table.

The two boxes: he stared at them now. His mother had packed them — her handwriting in black magic marker — and wrapped them in green waste bags that had kept the cardboard dry: 'books from apartment' and 'high school yearbooks'.

He'd forgotten about them when he packed his car for Everglades City, in a hurry to take his buddy Doobie up on his invitation: 'Stay with me while you look around. There's enough guide work for guys like us.' Meaning resilient soldiers who'd wrestled with the notion of liberation, helping the Iraqis so they could help themselves. Doobie had drawn a parallel: 'It's like me teaching fishermen to read the water and think like crocodiles.'

Michael ripped at the brown tape on the first box. Was it coincidence that he opened his senior yearbook to Carla's photo with the letter tucked inside? He'd never forgotten that they'd been in the same room when she secretly wrote it, and the next day mailed it.

'M— This first love won't last. We're practicing, trying things out. But you know I really really like you and yesterday when you carried that double scooper over, you licked it so the ice cream didn't soak the cone, you know how I hate that, and right then my heart tipped. Can you believe I wrote this when we were in my dad's den? Wasn't it great I could do it without you finding out? C—'

He'd left the letter lying on his dresser, and after that he stopped hiding his condoms in his bottom drawer.

That happened during the second and final year at

their vocational college where Carla had edged into the most prestigious crowd. They ran faster, stayed out later, took advantage of live music and good weed. Michael remained on the periphery, holding down two car mechanic jobs and thought, because he and Carla had made it out of high school together, they were on a firm footing. Until his father pointed out: 'Where'd the other Carla go? The smiley one with her hula hoop earrings?' Until she moved into an efficiency apartment and didn't need him around all the time.

Michael closed the box. Why drag all that up again? Didn't he have enough to cope with here?

He phoned his mother to say he'd stay one more night at the lake, then drive down to see her. He wanted to make it up to her: he'd driven straight from Florida to her Co-op where she worked, and stayed only for a sandwich before taking off for Cross Lake.

'How is your father?' she asked on the phone.

Like part of him wasn't there, but he wouldn't tell her that.

'Like he needs TLC.'

'Tender Loving Care. Of course.' Her words slow and thoughtful. 'I'll make spaghetti sauce and freeze it. Michael, can you talk him into a new cell phone?'

Tough moments, not easy, their separateness measured in miles and phone towers. Divorce was hard on everyone and he was not immune.

It was later than he'd intended when he drove into Cambridge. Automatically he glanced at his wrist, before remembering that he'd stopped wearing his watch, thinking it could relax him into his father's rhythm, so as not to push Jerry and make him more withdrawn than he already was.

The boat was the stalemate; it had been stored in Sam the truck driver's double garage all spring and summer. Big problem with the electricals – too big for Steele's skills.

Jerry on this shining lake without a boat, did that make sense? 'Dad, let's take it into one of those specialist marinas and get an estimate.'

Jerry had shrugged like a teenager who'd spent all of his allowance.

Things were slipping: the thought blew into Michael's head.

Winter was coming. There were jobs to do. On the surface Jerry behaved like they had all the time in the world, but underneath there was an edge of resentment – his voice low and jagged when he refused Michael's suggestions. No, he didn't want to cut branches that drooped over the roof. He didn't want to clean the trailer or air the mattresses outside while the weather held. It wasn't important the shower tray filled with water when they both used it. And his phone was good enough; nobody called him now anyway.

Michael recognized that tone of voice from Iraq: men holding it in when they needed to let it out.

Did he understand any better after he talked to Zac again on the phone?

'Mike, I'm telling you that bartender Renee was in the picture for a steady six months, but after the fire she was cut up and took it out on Jerry. Sure, he knew her house was empty that night and was smart enough to stay sober and hand his gun in when the sheriff showed up.' Zac's laugh was sharp. 'She didn't press charges and neither did Sandy. I heard Sandy's licking his wounds now and it's sad, your dad losing two friends at once. Drive west toward Loon Mission, you can see the foundations and the boathouse.'

So he did, on the way to Cambridge.

'Mom,' he called. 'You here?'

By the look of things, she'd been sitting at the table for a while. A jar with a candle inside burned on the counter and the room smelled of spaghetti sauce.

Edie picked up her glass. 'Join me. I'm on the Co-op's organic root beer.'

He leaned down to hug her. 'It's later than I planned.'

'I know. I got hungry.' An open stack of saltines lay on the table next to a jar of honey. His mother dug out a dab and ate it off the knife. 'You can do this when you live alone.'

'I'm here now.'

'For a few days.' She reached for a cracker and then put it back. 'How was it up there?'

'He lives on fried eggs and fish they keep in Dwayne's freezer. I made a pan of chili before I left, extra vegetables. Made sure he ate some.'

Edie May laughed. 'Well, it's spaghetti and salad for our special dinner. Do you still drink wine?'

'With you I do,' and he went to wash his hands.

'Your old moccasins are at the bottom of the stairs.' She stood up to boil the spaghetti water. 'The attic room is all ready for you.'

He called out: 'The doctor's room?'

'Hardly.'

Over dinner they both held back a little; they didn't know where the boundaries were. You couldn't exactly say to your mother: *What about boyfriends?* Or could you.

'Okay, Mom. Enough about work. What about men?'

'What about them?'

'The doc. Start with him.'

'Raoul helped me. You knew that.'

'Did anything happen?'

'No. He was… you know, a catalyst.'

'Did you want it to?'

'I don't know. Yes. I wasn't ready to move on, but I am now.' A long silence before Edie said, 'Michael, this isn't easy to talk about.'

'It's pretty weird for me to hear.'

'I'm old. If I started dating, I'd feel like an aging movie star making a comeback. With everybody watching.'

'Nobody's watching, Mom, and you look good. Those blonde streaks in your hair. I saw you at the Co-op. The staff respect you. They call you Edith.'

'I use my real name at work. I sort of like it.' She sighed. 'I miss you. How long can you stay?'

'Don't know. The boss said to phone him.'

'I'm always waiting for our next phone call. I'm good at waiting, but that doesn't mean I like it. Too patient,' she continued. 'That's me. Waited for Jerry to come back, then I waited for you. With you it was different.' She cocked her head. 'I couldn't watch the news every day. But this is what I did.

'I looked for people like me: waiters. When I went to the grocery store I'd sit on one of the old people's chairs and pretend to check my shopping list, but I scanned faces for other waiters.

'Once a man at the check-out handed over a box of cream puffs and said, My grandson's favorite, he's on his way home now. The army's let us know that much, and I thought: Believe it when you see him.' Edie shrugged. 'Everybody knows you can't freeze cream puffs.'

She pushed herself away from the table. 'I was jealous. Next time it's your turn.'

'To cook?'

'No. To talk. But let's take tomorrow off.'

He stayed four days and checked in with Jerry once. He phoned Ted who told him he could negotiate unpaid vacation, if he needed more than three weeks. He turned his attention to his mother, and didn't sleep badly. Everglades City faded and he let it fade.

His mother was as good as her word. The first day he worked on her car. On the second morning, they drove to the store for new windshield wipers and antifreeze. She said, 'But I'm not planning any long trips.'

'You drive down to the Cities. You might come and see me.'

'I knew you'd get around to that.'

'It's the drive, isn't it? So fly. I'll collect you in Miami if that's what you're worried about.'

'I don't know what I'm worried about,' she answered.

Over supper on the third night, she said, 'Okay. Carla.'

Michael took his time slicing into his pork chop. He'd learned in the army when not to act impulsively. 'What about her?'

'She shops in the grocery store on 9th Street every Tuesday and she shops at my Co-op on Friday mornings and has coffee in the bookshop.'

Michael stayed silently chewing.

'She buys a few treats for the weekend. You know.'

'No, but I can guess. Dougie still have lard legs?'

'I've only seen pictures.'

'Of kids?'

'Two. Both in school now.'

'And a dog.'

'In fact: yes. Big mangy thing named Milky. When he was a puppy, they fed him ice cream and called him Milky Wee.'

Which broke the ice. Michael laughed out loud, then wiped his mouth with his napkin and said, 'What's all of this information for, Mom? What's the point?'

'I think you have unfinished business with Carla. For one thing, she feels bad about how you broke up.'

'She said that?'

'Not exactly. But she always asks about you and last week she specifically said to say hello.'

'Big deal.'

'You haven't been serious about anyone since.'

'I was in Iraq.'

'You've been back almost three years.'

'I'm twenty-eight.'

'I know. This is your time.'

He looked into his empty glass. He should know better than to drink wine with his mother. But he walked over to the refrigerator for the bottle. Somewhere down deep, he knew she had a point. Then he heard her voice across the room.

'Did you think you'd be like me and your dad? Fall in love and get married. Because this is what I saw: first love, burned fingers. And I had to love you and love you because you were charred around the edges.'

'Like a piece of toast.'

'Please don't make fun. It was hard, watching you. All I'm saying is this is an opportunity to repair, hear what she's got to say. Michael, your first love doesn't have to be your only love.'

'That was *my* point to you. You might as well take your own advice.'

'I am, son. I'm getting out of the house more. I don't tell you everything, Mike. And you don't tell me everything, and that's all right. But I really would hate it if we stopped talking.'

'I guess we're in the same boat.'

'I guess we are.' Edie smiled. 'Is it Jerry's boat? What's it called? I hope you can get those repairs done, Michael. When he bought it, he towed it here to show me. Hung around for ages, talking.'

'Ya?'

'That was years ago. See if you can get him to sign the divorce papers, please?'

'If that's what you want.'

'I never wanted it, but I'm ready.'

His mother sat with her lips pressed together, something he hadn't seen for a long time, when she was about to cry. He looked away.

She said, 'I'm going to visit Rebecca soon. I'll let you know the dates and you can use the house.'

'I don't—'

'Just don't use my bedroom, okay.'

'Stop. That's enough.'

'It just might be.'

On the drive back to Cross Lake, Michael did not want to think about Carla Hoppe or his mother, but he did. Whatever happened, that dinner would be on his mind for a long time. It was the most intimate talking he'd done for years, as important as the night one of his men, on the verge of meltdown, walked into his room to talk at four am.

When his phone rang, he pulled over to take a call from Steele warning Michael that Jerry was manic, out by himself last night for a beer, but he'd scored something, speed, and so Dwayne and him had done shifts, walking Jerry around, trying to make him eat. But Jerry had an idea about staying awake all night to watch the sunrise.

Steele yawned: 'Think he'll sleep all afternoon. You can take over.'

'I'm on my way. I owe you one.'

'No you don't,' said Steele. 'We don't do it like that.'

Michael felt like the kid who couldn't put the puzzle together. There were rules to follow – and pieces everywhere, past and present, happy and sad, his father's genes, his own personality. What could he actually do for his old man?

But by the end of the drive, he'd found some strategies that helped him climb out. He found a radio station with sports highlights and country music, a girl DJ, sexy without trying too hard. He found bran muffins in the old-fashioned Swedish bakery, where the women wore scarves tied in back.

The girl who waited on him had a hard time with the box, tucking in the sides. When he ordered a coffee to go, the top wasn't on tight enough and she'd filled it to the brim and couldn't look at him. But he'd thanked her nicely and kept his thumb on the top until he was outside and could pour away some liquid and close it securely. We all have to learn, he thought. Sometimes it was more important to help someone save face than it was to be seen to be right.

That morning, after Michael had left, Edie accidentally knocked over the almost-empty orange juice carton on the breakfast table, then jumped up for a paper towel and kneeled down to wipe the floor, and glanced up to see, underneath her table, crayon marks – red and green and almost invisible yellow – and she stopped, shocked into the past, the unexpectedness of it, and burst into tears.

Edie stayed crying for a long moment and felt better for it, wiping her nose with the damp paper towel. 'That was me,' she said out loud, 'loving them too much. Nothing changes.' She still carried doubts about how she'd handled Jerry's moody silences; what to say when he didn't eat breakfast with them, just crept out to his shed before going to work. She'd had to explain, as best she could, that Daddy had bad dreams and it took him a long time to wake up.

Jerry's depression: the loneliness of it, how it isolated them, and Edie's panic that she might also lose her son. Now there was a name for it and leaflets from the Vets Administration that you could share with relatives. But then, even if there had been a support group for wives, Edie hated crying in public.

Sometimes she took coffee and toast outside and set it down by the shed door, softly calling his name, shivering in her bathrobe, her bare ankles. Sometimes she waited for an answer. Once, when she'd come back inside, Michael was underneath the table drawing: a yellow house without a shed and a red truck parked by the grass. 'Daddy going to work,' Michael had told her, 'in a new truck. Shhh, a surprise.'

Edie May had watched her ten-year-old son replace his crayons in their box, and pressed her lips together because where would the money come from, even for a newer second-hand truck?

It was as if her entire married life was written on that

kitchen table. She'd spent so much time sitting there and planning and peeling potatoes and making phone calls, it was as if their dreams, which were her dreams, had seeped through. Why had she kept this old table? Because she hung onto everything too long. Why hadn't she visited Michael in Florida? Because she'd have to face the fact that he loved it down there and planned to stay.

Michael took stock.

Outside, the shed door was open.

Around the trailer's window, the blue lights were on. Inside, his father was passed out on Michael's cot, shoes still on, feet hanging over the end, because he couldn't make it eight more steps to his own bed. Depressing.

He didn't want to waste energy looking at his father's world-weary face, so he gave him another hour to sleep, which would give Michael time to walk down near the harbor and check out Jerry's boat again, in Sam's garage.

Both the house and garage were closed up tight, which meant Sam was still on the road, but Michael had paid very close attention last week when Jerry pressed the code numbers on the keypad: 7779. It worked for him now. The tarp was still in a heap on the hood of the boat because Jerry, somewhere between embarrassed and disgusted, wanted to walk away from it, and so they did.

This time Michael climbed inside The Pikefinder — it was a matter of unscrewing the front panel to check the steering wiring. If he could rule out that loose connection, he'd be ahead of the game when they took it into a workshop. He'd already spotted Sam's toolbox.

This kind of work steadied him, always had, on cars

and now boats. He'd be glad to get back to Florida and learn more from Doobie and Ted; he missed them. But he was staying here for a while because if there was one thing Michael wanted to do, it was to get the boat running for spring. Whatever the cost, whatever the hassle. It would give his old man something to look forward to.

An hour later the soldier in him covered his tracks and put everything where he'd found it, then walked back to the trailer.

'Rise and shine. You're not sleeping all day.' Then he left the door open, letting in cold air.

Inside the shed, it looked like a maniac had been let loose. The cardboard boxes had been pushed across the room; one had split open, books spilling out. Fishing rods that had hung on brackets were strewn on the floor and the lawnmower was on its side as if Jerry was going to oil the blades before tackling his crabgrass one last time.

In the middle of the shed sat an old chest, and it took Michael a minute to recognize the cedar chest from the old house that had always been at the end of his parents' bed. It must have been moved from under the workbench. Now he opened it, the faint cedarwood scent rising up, along with the smell of winter gear, unwashed. Michael picked up a time warp of a jacket that his father had owned forever.

All those years ago, his father's plaid back going out the door; his mother at the stove. Hesitation in the air, as if he'd interrupted something. How she turned to ask 'Milk or juice?', but he'd already climbed off his chair. 'Don't go out there, you know it's off limits.' So it was a brave thing to do and, as he knocked, he glanced at the sandbox that he was too old for.

His father cracked open the door, looking down at him with that worried V between his eyes and said, 'Mickel Nickel', mispronouncing his son's name on purpose. Michael hoped for the magic trick: when a coin with the president's face appeared on his shoulder. But there were no nickels that day.

Michael shook his head to clear the memory.

Now when he stood up, he saw Jerry in the doorway. Bizarre timing.

'You've made a hell of a mess, Dad.' He said it calmly.

'So? Don't care.'

'You will tomorrow when the speed's out of your system.'

'What are you doing with my stuff?'

'Finding you a warm jacket.' You old fool, Michael thought. Did he say it out loud? 'So we can go for a long walk.'

'I'm going back to bed.'

'No, you're not. Not on my watch.'

'Go home. Take your boxes with you. I never wanted them.' Jerry lunged forward; Michael stepped to the right, doubting whether any punch his father tried now could really hurt him. Not like the one in the parking lot five years ago.

'Where's the rest of it, Dad? You've had enough.'

'Don't start.'

'Your body needs a break. Are there more pills in the truck?'

'I took a few painkillers; I was feeling no pain.'

'Let's get some food into you, that will help. Then we're taking a hike. I told Steele I was on duty, so you're stuck with me. Nobody said it would be easy coming down.'

So the day was not the write-off it might have been, that's how Michael saw it: coffee and eggs, a walk before dark, potatoes baked like hell in the oven. Jerry, bleary-eyed, watching TV in bed, with Michael at the table looking over Sunday's papers. Jerry reaching for a bottle inside his sleeping bag, his face sly, not contrite.

'What are you doing, Dad?'

'What is this, boot camp?'

'It won't hurt to stay dry for a few days.'

Jerry took a slug from the bottle. 'Rum never got anybody into trouble. Not when you think about the drugs that were around during the war. Yours too, I bet.'

'What's that got to do with you and me. Here and now?'

Jerry looked straight at him and said, 'I'm sick of your army voice. Try talking to me. Come on down to my level.' Then he turned the sound up on the television.

By ten-thirty the next morning Jerry's jacket had been sponged down and was drying upside down out the window of Michael's car, and Michael was talking his father into going for a run.

Jerry said, 'You don't think I can keep up. I'll show you, but I'm not doing this every day. How long you staying anyway?'

'Until we buy a clothesline and get the boat running.'

'I'm not spending all that money, so don't start giving orders.'

'We'll work something out about the cost. Hey, first run this week for me, too. We'll take it easy.'

It was a beautiful autumn. The clipped sunlight was hard to ignore. Michael jogged at a slower, steady pace, let Jerry sweat it out behind. After twenty minutes they'd doubled back by the boat harbor; Jerry walked the last of it.

Out front on Bachelors Road, Michael stood looking at the lake, duller, as if the rocks on the shoreline had shed a layer of dark red, purple, and the waves had mixed it in.

Jerry spoke first. 'Light's changing. Summer's over.'

'Did you get out much in Steele's boat?'

'After the mayflies stopped hatching, fish started biting.' Jerry smiled. 'Remember when you were first back and we took you out?'

Michael nodded. Clear and clean water. Walleye pike laying at the bottom of the boat, silver and sunlit. They'd fried them that night. 'I like it up here. Doesn't change much, does it?'

'The lake's always here. Old friend.'

Michael smiled at his father. 'I'm sorry about last night. I sort of reverted.'

'Sure did. You talk to your girlfriend like that?'

'Don't have one.'

'Why not? Sooner or later everybody gives in.' Jerry raised his arms and stretched. 'Hey, I don't feel too bad. I'm hungry.'

'That's good. Want to check out that new place, Freddy's? Their sign says food all day.'

Jerry slumped next to Michael in the round booth and scrutinized the menu. He kept his stocking cap on, though the place was warm.

'Cheese omelet will do me. Hash browns.'

Michael looked around for the server. 'Come on, Dad, order something different. What about a lunch special? When was the last time you ate turkey?'

'Renee cooked one for Easter. Slammed it into

Sandy's big oven.' His eyes brightened, then saddened. 'Don't play dumb. I know they filled you in on her.'

'A few facts.' Michael was relieved to see his father's feistiness, hoped he had more living to do. 'Anything you want to add?'

'Never used to buy pills in a bar. I was smashed. Don't know if I miss her or the Jacksona, it's all mixed up.'

'I went to look at the place. What's left.'

'Did you? What for?'

'I don't know. Seemed important.'

In between the forkfuls of meat and dressing, the men not looking at each other, an understanding was reached. The quality of the silence had shifted.

'While we're over here, let's stop at that pawn shop. You need a portable heater for the shed. We've got a few projects, Dad, besides the boat. Your vehicles need to be tuned up for winter. I want you safe and warm, if you're going to be digging cars out of ditches.'

'Ya, Ditch Dippers will keep me off the streets.' He smirked at his own joke.

'So don't lose any more weight, okay?'

Jerry, nodding, reached for the menu. 'Look at this, Mike. Turtle sundae. Remember those?'

'Where was that old-fashioned soda fountain, and Mom couldn't see why they were named that?'

'If you squint hard enough, they look like turtles.'

'Pecans — turn them on their backs, you see their heads.'

Jerry grinned, 'They serve them upside down in Missouri for good luck.'

A long time ago they'd conspired, fibbed. They'd swirled around on their stools, whooping it up, until Edie May told them to stop.

'She never liked scenes,' Mike said. 'Do you want one, Dad?'

'Not today.'

They stopped at the reception desk to pick up a card and ask about the marina.

Outside, they watched a car disgorge four hunters wearing camouflage and orange vests. 'No hunting,' Zac had said, meaning no guns around Jerry. It could be a long winter, Michael thought, without a clubhouse. And whatever thoughts his father had about last year and the warmth of a woman, he wasn't going to share them.

They took a look at the exterior of the lodge, laminate that looked like wood. Michael paused to find the joins. 'What about it, Dad? Make a cavity around the outside of the trailer, at least the side that faces the lake, then cover the insulation with this.'

'Sounds like work.'

His father was sleepy now, full of food. But Michael was determined to keep him awake, establish a normal routine. Jerry stayed in the car while Michael parked by the workshop attached to the marina. He took a good look around as he left his number with the mechanic, for a call back.

They walked into the small town of Onamia. The pawn shop flashed red lights. Only the pizza place was open.

'Ever tried this place?'

'Once,' Jerry answered. 'Renee and me. At the beginning. Let's go home.'

'Okay. Two more daylight hours. Feel like putting the shed back together?'

By dinnertime, they'd had a call from Freddy's foreman with the cost of servicing the boat. Major repairs would be itemized. Did they do installments? Not for new customers. Michael ended the call and said, 'I've got money, Dad.'

'A loan?'

'If that's what you want. Let's book her in.'

They raised a beer to the work they'd accomplished. But Jerry wanted a whiskey with a second beer chaser. Two steps forward, one step back, if Michael bothered to analyze it.

'Dad, we need to eat now. In town tomorrow we'll pick up food and liquor.'

'What else?'

'Clear out your post office box, pay bills. Let's tow the boat to Freddy's, then tackle your truck.'

'Don't talk to your mother about the boat. Not the details.'

He'd meant: the money. Old man had his pride. 'Understood. Anything else bothering you?'

'Maybe.'

Ten-thirty the next night: lights out. Michael, falling asleep, hears his father's voice:

'Okay, Mike, here's something. You didn't tell her that you had to come find me, did you?'

Michael groaned. 'Where are we talking about?'

'Everglades City.'

'Your visit last year?' Michael blinked and half sat up. The long car trip down; an overheated engine so Jerry stopped for a beer or three. Phoned Michael from the Magnet, which attracted loners and vets. Michael knew the bar, but it was a whole new trip to go there looking for your father.

'God, Dad, give me some credit. Why would I tell her

that?'

'Because you told her everything else, like I only stayed two nights.'

'No, I didn't. I skirted around a few things. Said you were worried about your car making the trip back. That was true.'

'She kept asking about your job. Couldn't figure out why I didn't go to work with you for an entire day.'

Michael sighed. If his mother had been his first Florida guest, it would have been easier – she would have liked his red living room with the sofa bed, his galley kitchen. Not big, not expensive, and nice and clean.

'It made me look dumb when she asked all about your apartment and was that girl still around.'

'Which girl?'

'The one who used to live there.'

'Mom's curious, all right. So I told her that girl had the cleanest hair in the world, because she left me a row of half-full shampoo bottles.'

'Ya?'

'But you wouldn't care about that. Or her note: 'These didn't work for me but I hate waste.' When I moved in, I told Mom because I knew she'd like the story, and then I ditched the note.' Michael paused, both of them mulling it over. 'I mean, it's not like I ever met her.'

'No?'

'Wish I had, though. Moved out of state. I kept her forwarding address for six months. Now get some sleep, okay?'

Michael lay and listened to the wind on the lake and his father's soft snoring.

It made him think how he got used to the lipstick walls and threw away the note because he was the kind of soldier who didn't keep letters very long, didn't share them. You got soft hanging onto mementos. So he'd thrown all but one of his mother's careful cards and Jerry's scrawled notes, unintentionally funny.

His parents' mismatched communication. He'd never worried before about what he said to who. Jerry – a little paranoid, and stubborn. Edith – lonely, trying hard not to pry. He'd not wanted to take such a close look at them or gauge the passage of time.

Michael turned onto his side, feeling something like nostalgia or homesickness. Had he ever thanked his father for writing? His parents now were so real. And Carla was real. What did she look like? Was she happy?

On the edge of sleep, important questions had been let loose.

Then Michael did what he always did to calm down and let go. He concentrated on the work for tomorrow: exercise, hardware store, post office, workshop. It was better than counting sheep.

Anything that had gone into the trailer could come out and be scrubbed.

The way Jerry saw it, that was bullshit. Killing spiders wasn't part of the bargain. He stood with his arms crossed, defending his territory.

The compromise: leave the bed and TV. Everything else out, including the mattresses so that the walls and floor could be washed, the shower and cupboards wiped down – while checking for mouse holes and sealing the edges where the walls met the floor. Get it all done in one sunny day.

The next morning Jerry watched the rain come down, with satisfaction.

Sam the truck driver walked up to see them. He was back home for a while, surprised that the boat and trailer were gone, but his garage was swept out, so he'd wanted to thank them. Sam removed his work glove to shake hands with Michael, then called a garage party. He'd brought beer and brandy and real pecan pie, not too sweet, back from the Deep South and planned to defrost his freezer, dig out some venison.

'Bring your own silverware and steak sauce,' Sam said.

Five men and a dog sitting in Sam's garage in a semicircle looking out at the rain. Steele, Queenie, Dwayne, Jerry, Michael, Sam – a beer in their hands or down by the chair – jackets buttoned up to the neck, as if they were waiting for winter.

It was around the corner, somebody said. The talk turned to ice fishing and last year's plowed road from the Jacksona right out on the lake.

'Anyone heard from Sandy?' Sam asked, and there was a moment of silence for something or someone long gone. 'Nobody hunting?' When he received an evasive answer from Dwayne – the county had made it harder to get a license this year – Sam simply nodded.

Michael told them how they were waiting for an estimate on the boat repairs and Jerry bragged about how easy it had been to hook up The Pikefinder and tow her over. His truck was working pretty good.

'What are your plans, Mike?' Sam wanted to know. 'How long you around?'

'Till we know the damage on the boat. But I'm heading back to Cambridge this afternoon, in fact, for a few days. So keep an eye on the old man? He's starting to feel cocky about his run in the morning.'

Steele said, 'I heard they don't work fast over there. If you're not around when they finish, we'll make sure the boat comes back, all in one piece.'

And Michael kept his thoughts about leaving the boat outside all winter to himself. Maybe they would figure something out.

Sam set the food out on his workbench and they helped themselves to sliced tomatoes, coleslaw, and roast cut into chunks that would fit on forks. They ate with their plates on their laps, slowly, nowhere to go.

Dwayne walked back to his trailer to find the tub of ice cream left from summer.

Michael offered to wash the plates and silverware, which made them laugh.

When Sam served up pie and ice cream, Jerry said, 'In Missouri, they turn pecans over for good luck. Everybody knows that.'

'I don't,' said Sam.

Michael laughed. 'It's an old joke and not strictly true. But hey—', he raised his shot of Southern Comfort, 'to Bachelors Road. Thanks for having me.' Then he turned to his father. 'Next week we'll clean out the trailer and winterize the truck.'

'The kid and his checklist.'

But Michael heard the hint of pride. They all would have.

Edie May opened her door to Michael, smiling.

He hugged her and told her she smelled great.

'But how do I look? Notice anything different?'

'Your hair?'

But she laughed and said, 'New sweater. For the bright lights of the city, and a party. Two nights away,

Michael, and please stay at least one more night when I return. Then we'll talk. I want to hear all about the Bachelors.'

The place to himself – even if it was a mattress on the floor. The keys were on the table along with a note:

'Meatloaf in the fridge. Don't let it go to waste...
Details you might want: Tuesday – in town 9th St, time varies. Friday – a.m. Co-op, bookstore
p.s. You know I don't pay attention to cars – blue'

The car information was new. He'd already made a point of memorizing the days and times, potentially useful details. Was it coincidence that today was Monday? He hadn't really thought about it, all the days on Bachelors Road were pretty much the same.

Michael sat at the kitchen table and stared at the meatloaf sandwich. He lined up his thoughts so they didn't whirl. He'd hear what she had to say. People don't really change but everyone moves on in their own way. If it was chit-chat, he wouldn't stick around long.

Michael drained the water in his glass. He watched his hand push it away, across the nicked and scarred surface of the table. His hand was changing into his father's hand, a little weathered. But his father's hands were remarkably steady, his eyesight still sharp, when they'd put the lawnmower back together, collected the screws and bolts on the floor. If Jerry kept up the running, cut out the booze, put on some weight, in a year he could... what?

He kept staring. Was it easier to turn his thoughts to his father than to stand back and look at himself? His hand – not old, not young, the nails needed trimming and his clipper was in his wash bag. The bathroom to himself. He'd like a bath, hot as hell, and this was his chance to lay back on that funny plastic pillow in the shape of lips.

Michael had already spotted the blue car. He was a parking lot stalker. He'd never tell anyone, not even Doobie, about this.

The grocery store shared the back lot with the hardware store. The Swedish bakery, with the red-faced girl serving coffee, was a block away. He'd walk there later and drown his sorrows. He sat in his car, waiting, and felt like an idiot; then tried a nonchalant walk in the back door. He blinked. Dim lighting and no frills equaled low prices. People shopping, working.

She wasn't there – and then she was. It was the way she stood with her left leg twined around her right, contemplating the canned goods section. In profile: gaze steady, hair longer. Beautiful in baggy jeans.

Did she feel him watching? Because she turned and said, 'Guess it wasn't hard to find me. I'm so predictable. You look great.'

'You too. Your hair's lighter.'

'I'm a hairdresser, remember?' She smiled. 'But mostly I'm a housewife.'

'You don't work?'

'Thursdays and Saturday mornings.' She looked at him steadily. 'I'm happy to see you. Come over for lunch.'

'When?'

'Now,' she laughed, and pointed to the packet of hot dogs in her cart, the block of cheese. 'I still make angels-on-horseback, but only for a treat. You liked the onion chopped up fine.'

Suddenly he was in back of her, hands on her waist,

scarcely breathing. 'Let's go.'

'I have things on my list, Michael. I need everything to look normal.'

'Do you?'

'Of course.'

As they walked around, he relaxed a little as they talked. She asked about Jerry and Cross Lake, and Florida. He told her about his job only a mile away from his apartment, and the fishing. Carla told him about looking up Edie May at the Co-op, how she liked sitting in the bookshop for an hour on Fridays, time to herself before the weekend took over.

Then they changed their plan because Forest Lake was twenty minutes away. It was a better use of time to drive both cars to Edie May's on Tacoma Avenue. Carla had to leave at two o'clock at the latest. Like she'd done this before, he thought. He bought a bag of ice and helped himself to an empty cardboard carton to make a cool box so nothing spoiled. It gave him something practical to do.

In the parking lot they transferred the perishables to her car and covered the box with a towel.

'Kids – always getting dirty, not to mention car sickness.' She shrugged. 'I've only been to Edie May's once so I'll follow you.'

On the way, he stopped himself from glancing too often in his rearview mirror.

They sat together on the couch.

Carla said to him, 'Tell me about your bachelor pad with fancy TV.'

'I like sports, news, and my place is small so the screen is mid-size. I don't want it to dominate.'

'What do you want to dominate?'

The bedroom, he thought, but didn't say.

Carla looked around the living room. 'These blue floorboards. I admire Edie's style, for sure. She and I are friends, Michael. I like her, always did. Now we've switched places. She's single, I'm married. Never thought it would turn out like this.'

'When Mom told me about your Christmas cards, it threw me. It was weird.'

'But today's not so weird, is it?' She reached for his hand. 'Doug and I are okay. We're doing the best we can.' She paused. 'We go to church, Michael. It's modern with bongo drums and poetry. They have prayer slips. You fill one in and the congregation prays for your intention for a week.'

He looked at her: grown-up Carla.

'When you were in Iraq, I thought of you. And your mom talks about your dad sometimes so Jerry gets my vote often.' She turned Michael's wrist over to see his watch. 'I don't want lunch. Can we just lie down so I feel close to you?'

Upstairs, he watched Carla smile at the bare bones of it: mattress with blankets pulled tight, one rug and a lamp, a clothes rail in the corner with winter coats in plastic bags.

She sat on the mattress and pulled off her boots.

And he began: 'It's sort of a blur, that last fight.'

'It wasn't a fight. I said that you never talked to me anymore.'

'I was working two jobs, putting in the hours for the certificates.'

'I know that now. But I was bored, Michael.'

'How could you be, all those parties in your apartment?'

'It was an efficiency, only big enough for a few friends.'

'Lying all over the floor.'

'It was my living room. We were living.'

'So I couldn't go to bed. You didn't care. You didn't start work until ten.'

She stayed silent, not protesting.

He'd surprised himself with that memory and his anger, unfurling. He'd walked out that night, too young and hurt to talk it through.

She'd never given him a key, so he had nothing to return. Two weeks later she'd left a shoebox by his front door – high school ring, sunglasses, travel clock, heart-shaped rock from Lake Superior – and a pillowcase filled with laundry.

'My dirty laundry, Carla. That was low.'

'I felt bad about that. Always. It's on my Regrets List. I am so sorry.'

They looked right at each other and then she smiled. 'Thank God I've apologized.'

Something was completed for her. He saw it as she sat back on the mattress with her legs stretched out.

She said, 'We talked in bed. That's where you felt safe.'

'I guess so.' He was thinking about his father, in the dark talking about Florida, how those doubts had doubled up in Jerry's mind, how afterwards he'd slept like a baby. Not much in life worked that way. He said, 'I've got more of Jerry in me than I want to recognize.'

'Do you?'

'I like Cross Lake. But I couldn't take it full time.'

'Don't rush away, Michael. They both love that you're here. And come back sooner. Why leave it so long?'

Carla crawled off the mattress and picked up her

boots. At the top of the stairs she hugged him. 'We are lucky, all of us. A place to rest with a roof for refuge.'

'Sounds like you could read that out at church. Maybe leave my name out of it.'

Carla laughed. 'There's nothing to hide. I mean, you could come over sometime. Now look, I want to trim your hair before I leave.'

Then she was gone, back to her family, taking her smile and scissors with her. He'd miss her for a while, how long?

The last thing Carla had asked: 'What else could you do for them before you go?'

He phoned the foreman at Freddy's, said that his father would be paying the final bill, but he'd like to send a check now to cover the first half. 'It's a gift, so don't say anything. Just put the balance on my dad's invoice.'

Michael liked to get the difficult things out of the way. He left his phone on the table and went for a long run. Then he raked leaves, and the next day he walked to the Co-op, bought a book and sat outside with hot soup and read. The cars in the parking lot pulling in and reversing, the traffic light changing, the ordinary hum of life was a comfort.

Edie May noticed her son's haircut right away and so he told her that he and Carla talked and it was sort of a relief.

Rebecca's party was a success and the charming man who'd been invited to meet Edie May looked disappointed when she'd excused herself to circulate. It was good to know that men like him were around, although his separation was recent, much too recent.

'Speaking of,' she added, 'the divorce papers. Any progress on that front?'

'We emptied his PO box, but most of his mail is sitting in the shed.'

Edie May sighed. 'I've waited this long and there's only so much I can ask of you. I guess I need more fluidity.'

'Nice word, Mom.'

'But do you have time to drop by Rebecca's on your way back?'

He saw it clearly: she wanted her family together once in a while. 'I'll try. And what about that Florida break this year?'

What was left in the remains of the Jacksona fire: a stack of cheap, fake wood melamine bowls. Michael fished them out of the rubble as he and Jerry walked down to the lake.

'For popcorn,' Jerry nodded. 'Nice old popping machine.' He paused. 'Renee took it easy with the salt, wasn't going to trick us into getting thirstier.'

They stood by the shoreline. The lake was colorless, odorless, preparing to freeze. Jerry paced around. Michael walked out on the dock to take a look at the boathouse, the letters spelling out the name, white and brazen.

'New paint, Dad?'

'August. My contribution to the clubhouse.'

'You're lucky that you've still got the lake, Dad.'

'Nobody can take that.'

Michael half smiled at his father: 'That was one thing about Iraq – the night sky, knowing there was a universe out there and wanting to be part of it.'

'Ya, only a speck, but part of something. I get that feeling here.'

They picked up the bowls and skimmed them like stones. Whose flew the furthest? They watched them fill with water, tilt and sink. Jerry said, 'Did I tell you about the time capsule that I buried with Zac? Couldn't find it last summer. When you're coming this way again, we should get Zac up here and try again.'

'I'd like to see him.' Michael knew that Zac was the best friend his dad had. 'It's been too long.'

'We'll do it then if you've got the time.'

'I do,' Michael said. 'Definitely.'

A NOTE ON THE AUTHOR

Candyce Lange began writing creatively in high school. She writes poetry as well as fiction. Her work has appeared in *Stand*, *The North*, *The Interpreter's House*, the *Fenland Poetry Journal* as well as in Poetry Wivenhoe anthologies. She currently lives in Ely, Cambridgeshire and contributes poetry reviews to sphinxreview.co.uk.

Made in the USA
Monee, IL
17 April 2021

66068728R00090